Buying the Duke's Silence
(Ladies of Inspiration: Book 2)

by Jeanna Ellsworth

Check out Jeanna Ellsworth blog and other books by Hey Lady Publications: https://www.heyladypublications.com
Follow Jeanna Ellsworth on Twitter: @ellsworthjeanna
Like her on Facebook:
https://www.facebook.com/Jeanna.Ellsworth
Connect by email: Jeanna.ellsworth@yahoo.com

Dedication

To my daughter, Madison, who has endurance and passion enough for the both of us. You encourage and inspire the best parts of me to shine when others have tempted me to change.

Acknowledgements

For so many years, I feared being invisible. Like all of humanity, I simply wanted to be seen; seen for who I was, who I had become, and the potential inside of me that I had not yet explored. Over the last two and a half years, as I struggled with a bit of work/life balance issues, I had to learn to fight for my writing time.

No matter what it was that diverted me from writing, I knew it was me that resisted sitting still long enough to write. You see, it wasn't writers block that slowed this book from publication, because when I finally did sit down, it poured out of me. Even my angst or worries of the day dripped away. The reward in writing was there, so why did I struggle to make time to write?

As many of my loyal readers and friends can attest, my books are often snapshots of who I am. I believe that I resisted writing because I was afraid to see myself. I felt invisible, and yet, there was a part of me that I didn't dare share. There were sacred parts of me that were only known to me; the hurt, the lessons from my choices, and the growth that came from painful experiences.

The irony was that I feared being invisible, yet was afraid to show who I was. Repeatedly, close friends and family, as well as readers, begged for more "me".

I'd like to acknowledge and thank those who desperately wanted to see me become less invisible and heavily encouraged my writing over the last months: Richard B., Stacey F., Christy B., Melanie S., Bryce C., Ron P., Patsy P., Donna C., Betsy W., KaraLynne M., Tiffany W., Kim H., Sean D., Yester B., Karen M., and Bethany M.

There are many more I could list, but most of all, thank you to my readers. When you read my books, ponder them, or recommend them, you are encouraging me to write, just like those I'm intimately acquainted with.

The reception of "me" has been overwhelming. Interestingly, this book was written using my daughter, Madison

Ellsworth, as the main character, whose initials happen to be M. E.— Me. Many say she looks the most like me, and that is incredibly flattering, because she is stunning. You can see for yourself, she is on the cover. Those who know her will agree that she is one of the greatest people on earth. Recently, I heard her friend say those very words. So thank you, Madison, for being the kind of heroine that is worthy of such praise.

I'd also like to take a special moment to thank my dear friend and fellow author, Melanie Schertz. Multiple times, she has pulled me from my darkest moods, and within minutes, I have laughed so hard, I cried. Most recently, I have understood one thing about her that is priceless. She is the paragon of knowing how to accept who you were, who you have become, and the potential inside that has not yet been explored.

BUYING THE DUKE'S SILENCE

PROLOGUE

Early December 1818

"Evelyn, you cannot neglect this opportunity to impress the new Marquess of Tisdale. He was already an earl, but now a marquess! My daughter, a marchioness— He certainly showed you preference the last few weeks. What fortune that his uncle died, leaving him a fortune and two titles. You must further earn his regard and get him to propose. Must I repeat that last sentence?" Her mother's eyes were set and each word was punctuated with emphasis.

Evelyn Hughes let out a slight giggle and shook her head. The intensity with which her mother was telling her to marry the marquess was weighted heavy in drama.

Three weeks ago Mr. Grey, as that was his name then, started calling on Evelyn three times a week. He always overstayed the typical time for a visit, and had warmed her English Mastiff's protective nature nearly overnight. Evelyn's three-year-old dog, Honeymae, no longer barked her deep intimidating bark, and instead would snuggle her muzzle into his hip until Mr. Grey scratched and cooed at her.

Her gentle giant never left her side with other visitors, frequently growling at them until they were so anxious they left. Not so with Mr. Grey. It was the one thing that calmed Evelyn. Honeymae was a very protective dog and had a way of knowing whom to trust.

She reminded herself that he wasn't "Mr. Grey" anymore. He was the Marquess of Tisdale.

Just saying his name in her head brought his image to her mind. He was tall, taller than any man she had ever danced with, and had straight jet-black hair that shone in the candlelight. He always combed it back and slicked it with waxed pomade, which tickled her nose with its distinctive scent of cloves and reminded her of apple cider at harvest time. He always had minty fresh breath, too. His eyes were dark, so much so that there was no delineation between the iris and the pupil, and they shimmered as well.

It was true that the Marquess of Tisdale had shown her marked preference over the last few weeks, even reserving the waltz at every ball they attended. It made her heart speed up just thinking about being in his arms in such a near embrace. He still kept to the original waltz position where opposite hands were joined above the head, creating a seemingly secluded arch. But because of his height, he always held her closer than other gentlemen so that the arch did not fatigue her arm.

Returning to the conversation, she said, "Yes, Mamma. I cannot think of anyone I would rather marry than Mr. Harrison Grey—I mean, Lord Tisdale." She held back the feeling of a girl in a candy shop. "I do hope I shall not make the mistake with his name tonight. It will be the first time I will see him with his newly inherited titles. Do I have to call him 'The Most Honorable Marquess of Tisdale'?"

"No, dear, the full title is only used when he is announced at a ball, but you can just call him Lord Tisdale, or 'My Lord'. His earldom is too meaningless to even address. And who wants to be called the Earl of Wimperton? What an awful name. He should be grateful that his marquess outranks that title."

Her mother clapped her hands and said, "My daughter, Marchioness of Tisdale! You will be so wealthy, and be called—" she paused for effect, "'—My *Lady*'."

Her mother's voice got stern again. "Do not mess this up. Do not let your feeble heart get carried away with sentiment. I am having enough trouble with your sister and her weakness for penniless third sons with no profession." Her mother sent a pointed look at her sister, Ester, who was desperately trying to hide the pain that comment caused.

Mrs. Hughes patted the red curls that crowned Evelyn's head and kissed the top of her forehead. "I am so proud of you. Do not disappoint me. Do whatever he asks of you."

Her normally soft-spoken sister Ester spoke up. "Mother! You do not really mean that!"

"Why ever not? If he compromises her, he has to marry her!" Mrs. Hughes looked at Evelyn in the mirror and said, "Now be a good girl and do what I say. Mother always knows best." She then sent a dark look to Ester and repeated herself. "Mother *always* knows best. I have never led you astray. I have lived, and therefore have known. Experience buys respect. And I know you respect me."

Evelyn placed an obedient smile on her face to appease her mother. Mrs. Hughes then left their chambers.

She had learned that her mother valued honor and respect more than any other thing, but what was the harm in such principles? It meant Evelyn was trained and polished to make a brilliant match in her first season. It meant that she was prepared to succeed in life, to be admired and respected, just like her mother.

She had been trained since birth for this moment in her life. All that her mother ever taught her in life led to finding a wealthy husband. A good, smart match was all she was ever taught.

For your name was how people know you.

Now was the time to put all of her hard work into action. She had to win the Marquess of Tisdale.

She trusted most of what her mother had just said, although there was one sliver that was raw with ache. Not just for her, but for her sister, too. Evelyn wasn't surprised that her sister Ester had been slighted so blatantly for loving someone other than a marquess.

The pattern had been set years ago. Evelyn was not to offer Ester pity.

Her mother had left the room, so it did not stop Evelyn from offering empathy. "Do not listen to her harshness, Ester. She will be persuaded, then you and Phillip can get married. I promise you that I will get the Marquess of Tisdale to propose, then it will not matter one wink that Phillip is a third son. I shall have all the money you need to live. You will get what your heart imagines."

Ester blushed a bit and looked up through her eyelashes and smiled. "Mrs. Phillip Thomas, how well that sounds. He is everything I want! I would never be happy with any other man.

Oh, do marry the marquess, if only to get Mother and Father to lighten the pressured thumbs and give us permission to marry!"

"I promise to do everything in my power to do so. I'll be Lady Tisdale by the New Year."

Evelyn had never been so committed to a thing in her life, if for any other reason than to let Ester be happy with Phillip.

But how do you trap a marquess?

*****

Kenneth Silence was ready for something new in his life. He had finished his last project with Lord Klassen two weeks ago, but no new work had been requested of him. At least none that was interesting. His best friend, Gavin, the Duke of Huntsman, was still on his wedding trip with Grace and that meant his night held two options: stay home and review the new letters of business and decide which work to accept, or go to the Halliburtons' dinner party.

Usually he was not one to turn down socializing with all the debutantes, but recently he had become tired of the blonde-haired, blue-eyed ladies with perfectly curled hair batting their eyelashes at him innocently. Examining him north to south, occasionally a slight delay at the equator, and then north again. As if they wanted to lick him. Up until recently it had never been received in a repulsive way.

The game was feeling antiquated. Overused. Worn out. The days and nights had become habitual. Not truly memorable, as it was just one lady from the next.

He wanted someone who left an impression. Perhaps he wanted one with a bit of impertinence, who was not afraid to speak an original thought. One who was not superficial. But an intelligent, original mind was only one part of what he truly desired. In his line of work, deceit ran rampant. Greed and selfishness, too. So, lately he felt this intense need to find a lady who would sacrifice something great for something better.

14

Someone who could love passionately. Loyally. The search was burning him out.

He laughed at himself because, sadly, he truly hadn't been looking all that long.

He adjusted his office chair behind his desk and opened the day's correspondence.

The first request he opened was to help a rich widow find a bitch for her ailing King Charles Cavalier to mate with.

His insides cringed, even making one of his eyes twitch tighter as he flinched.

Is that what his investigation skills had come to? Is that all he was good for?

Suddenly he burst out laughing for a second time. His butler, Jenkins, came in and asked, "Sir? Is everything well?"

Kenneth just bellowed harder, thinking of the request to find a particular breed of dog, and this widow was willing to pay him to do so!

But it correlated so well to his plight. He couldn't stop the tears from coming. Here he thought he was stepping away from finding a female by avoiding the Halliburtons' dinner party.

He caught his breath and raised his eyebrow once or twice suggestively, lifting the letter. "I have been hired to find a bitch of superior breeding, with hair like a fawn and who is willing to enter into the family way!"

Jenkins smiled, but managed to hold back the chuckle. "I shall have Richards set aside your dinner jacket. I see you are going to the Halliburtons' after all."

*****

In no time at all, Kenneth Silence was dressed and walking the half-mile to Halliburton Manor. Carriages were plentiful, which meant it was well-attended. He really should be very grateful that he had been invited. The Halliburtons were a very respectable family known for their poised, but generous, nature. They always offered superior entertainment afterwards, often hiring professional singers and musicians. He knew that tonight would not be any different.

He removed his hat as he climbed the steps. Mrs. Halliburton greeted him first. "Oh, Mr. Silence! How delighted I am that you have come. There are many young ladies here who I know would love to hear the tales you spin. Our party would not have been the same if you had stayed home." Her sincerity was a reprieve from most of the *ton*.

"Please, Mrs. Halliburton. Just call me Silence. Mr. Silence was my father, may the devil rest his soul, but I should hate to be mistaken for him. Not to mention that I do hope my father's soul stays at rest, wherever that may be!" He then winked at her.

She let out a genuine laugh that brought a sparkle to her eyes, and her matronly belly jiggled in a way that most ladies of society would have been repulsed by. "Of course, Silence, but I always find it such a contrasting name to your character. For anyone who knows you knows that silence is the first thing that leaves the room once you enter!"

He bowed, kissed her hand, then wiggled his eyebrows flirtatiously. "And that is the beauty of my name."

She blushed brightly. "Indeed! Now, please go enliven the drawing room. You will find several beauties you are well acquainted with."

Kenneth pretended to be disappointed. "Well, that has no draw for me."

She giggled. "You are such a dandy. Very well, go procure someone to introduce you to those you do *not* know. I shall welcome the last of my guests and will soon follow."

Kenneth winked again to her, thinking to himself, *Challenge accepted.*

He entered the room, appearing to scan like all other socialites, nodding greetings and acknowledging those whom he must.

Three men had canes, another carried a dress sword on his right hip, but the way he slouched to the side as if it was too heavy meant the sword was only for looks, and Kenneth assumed he did not know how to use it. There was another gentleman with his back to him, with a suspicious bulge that could be a pistol. He would have to keep an eye on him. There were two exits, both on the east, one of which he just had entered from. The bookshelf may possibly have a trap door, for there were newer carved marble moldings in the center shelves with a slightly different grain than the pillars in the center of the room.

He didn't mean to survey a room in this manner, but knowing the potential perils, the obstacles, the room layout, and the tools at his disposal were part of his job. He had to know who were the men he could trust, and who he could not.

He continued to scan the room. Three ladies were grouped together, with no gentlemen talking to them. *Ah, wallflowers. The best kind.*

He made his way there but was stopped by Mr. Grey. "Silence! You made it after all!"

He caught the eye of one of the wallflowers, smiled charmingly, and then turned to the new Marquess of Tisdale. "I suppose I must call you 'My Lord' now. Right, Grey?"

Lord Tisdale appeared slightly sad, but his eyebrows pinched together and his upper lip twitched. Whatever he was about to say was not the truth. "It is such a sad way to earn a title. A loved one must die to gain it."

Kenneth Silence was very good at finding out the truth with his line of questioning, which made him a very good investigator when others so desperately wanted to find solace in falsehoods, but he also had an uncanny ability to tell when someone was lying. It wasn't anything specific, and probably wasn't much more than noticing changes in body language or the tone of voice, but to Kenneth it felt like an art form that he continually perfected. It was enough to know that Lord Tisdale did not necessarily mean his words. At least not entirely.

Unfortunately, he couldn't always let on that he knew that they were lying. So he said, "Yes, it is so sad that your uncle died so unexpectedly. It brings some solace to know that he left you well cared for."

The marquess' voice shook slightly, but with forced emotion. "I do not like to speak ill of the dead, but it should have been my father to inherit it. You know how he was, though, at the tables. My father would not have made a good marquess, for the fortune would have been gone in a fortnight." His voice had arched slightly as he said the last sentence, which meant it was another falsehood. "If only he hadn't cheated that last game and been forced to duel two summers ago. At least that is the story that my uncle shared before he died."

"Well, Tisdale, as I suppose I must call you now, you do not have to act too disappointed. You have earned a great deal of attention since earning your title. Speaking of which, there is a stunning redhead beckoning you. Might you introduce me?"

Tisdale turned and genuinely smiled at the beauty, who was blushing brightly as she saw them approach.

As the distance between them narrowed, he noticed what fine features she had. Her hair was not quite a brilliant red and yet not quite blonde, but seemed to have streaks in it as if the sun had bleached it and it couldn't make up its mind which color to be. But it was definitely more red than blonde.

Her eyes were more deeply set than many, but he was never a fan of large eyes. They made him think of his mother and one cannot have daydreams about eyes like your mother.

As he got even closer, he noticed the subtle freckles that dotted her petite rounded nose and cheeks. Her cheekbones were high and flushed with natural color. Her chin was feminine yet her jaw was slightly angled, drawing his eyes to her neck, which nearly made him blush.

Hold your ground.

He glanced back to her and could see the length and smoothness of her neck created the impression of a precious piece of art on display on a pedestal; her unique and very memorable face.

He had used the word "stunning" when asking for an introduction, but even that was not nearly adequate to describe her.

Being this close to her left him rather breathless, and he hoped he would be able to speak when the time came.

Finally, a lady who is able to reduce me into living up to my name.

Tisdale started the introductions. "Miss Hughes, allow me to introduce you to Kenneth Silence. Silence, this is Miss Hughes."

He bowed deeply, yet not so deep that he was forced to drop his gaze. "The pleasure is all mine, Miss Hughes." And he meant it. Being this close to her was truly a pleasure.

Miss Hughes looked at him with powder blue eyes and a polite smile, but quickly turned back to Tisdale. "You know so many people, My Lord. How shall I know whom to trust?"

Kenneth did not fail to notice that she didn't even greet him.

Perhaps she was not as attractive as he once thought, or had not been raised in polite society.

Tisdale chuckled and replied, "Blast if I know who to trust! Forgive me. I should not have cursed."

"There is nothing to forgive, Lord Tisdale. I trust that whoever you introduce me to is someone very important. A marquess would never associate with someone who is not of the first waters."

Miss Hughes finally spoke to Kenneth. "And what do you do?"

So she assumed he was a man of business, and not titled. It was true, he wasn't, but he was still a gentleman. He used his usual form of escape for those in the *ton* he no longer wished to associate with. "Me? Oh, I leech off of good men like Tisdale to procure and encounter—"

She cut him off and, while placing her hand flirtatiously on Tisdale's arm, said, "You are quite correct, he is an excellent gentleman."

She continued with the silky words and, slowly, the sweet smile appeared waxed. And the light in her eyes held shadows.

Kenneth had believed she was a beauty at first, but her simpering up to the marquess was certainly enough to make him ill.

His attempts to excuse himself went unheard.

But he was delighted to find that Mrs. Halliburton was motioning him toward the three ladies, the wallflowers, he had spotted earlier.

He was introduced to all of them: Miss Kelly Martin, Miss Elizabeth Dobson, and Miss Loraine Kissinger. He made small talk with them for the next few minutes, offering sincere compliments and enjoying seeing each one blush. One of them even took out her fan and started fanning herself.

Kenneth knew he was a flirt, but he did not ever offer falsehoods. How could he? A man who could tell truth from lies found a great deal of solace in telling the truth. So often, he was forced to pretend he believed the lies to maintain his friendships in the *ton*, or to get the information he sought. But with ladies like these wallflowers, they hadn't yet learned the art of false flattery. So when they spoke of how they enjoyed the lemonade, it usually meant they enjoyed the lemonade. Honest answers made his nearly constant headache go away.

The conversation between them continued and he found he was truly enjoying himself. However, before too long, he recognized Miss Hughes' voice whispering behind him.

There was something about whispering that made Kenneth's ears perk up. Perhaps it was the innate investigator in him, perhaps it was his natural curiosity to know the truth, but nevertheless he always found himself listening. True whispers were always honest. Sure, there were the rumoring whispers—meant to be overheard—but those were easy enough to weed out. These whispers behind him were of the secret kind, the kind that was meant to be between two people and no one else.

He felt a bit of guilt for listening, but that did not stop him. It rarely did. He was an information gatherer. People hired him for this reason.

Miss Hughes' voice was low. "He seemed the same as before he got the titles. I shall have to do everything I can to get him to propose tonight."

The other lady whispered, "He is so rich now! And titled!"

"Do not forget handsome."

The two ladies giggled quietly and the other lady asked, "How could you ask for anything more?"

"I cannot. There is no better match for me than Lord Tisdale. I will be so admired when I am Marchioness of Tisdale. Mark my words, I will outrank every female in this room by the end of the month. Quickly, it looks like they are calling us for dinner; I want to be near him so he can escort me in."

With that the two ladies hurried away, clueless to the fact that Kenneth heard their fortune-hunting plans.

He would have to warn Tisdale.

*****

During the separation of the sexes, Kenneth took Tisdale aside and explained what he had heard as gently as possible.

The man seemed to not be disturbed in the slightest. "Not to worry, chap; I have had my sights set on her for some time now. Perhaps I will let her compromise me—how enjoyable that would be—and then my mother will insist she marry me to preserve my reputation!"

Kenneth was relieved to hear that there was some regard on Tisdale's part. "What reputation? If anything, I would hope you would want to build a new reputation!"

"Touché!"

"Well, it sounds like she would welcome such a chance to do just that!"

"Ah, and the chance would be pure pleasure for me. But would you like to place a wager on how far she would go to win me?"

Kenneth didn't like that thought, so he said, "No, I will not bet on it, but I should like to know your plans all the same." There were times Kenneth relished being honest.

Tisdale tipped his head down and lowered his voice. "Here is the secret. She cannot sing. For all that beauty, and what a sight to look at, too—lord, I wish I could bed her—she has no talent for music. Sure, she can play a tune here or there if she has the music, but her voice would rival the screech of a hawk hunting its prey. Or maybe it is more like a bear waking up from hibernation. No, perhaps it is a mixture of breaking glass and a crackling fire. I do not know how to describe it, but her voice is offensive to the ears."

Tisdale shook his head in disbelief, or emphasis, one of the two. "I will be punishing myself, but you just watch; I will get her to sing tonight. She will do anything to please me."

Kenneth only saw truth in his words, which only made him force a polite smile. "That bad? And does she know she cannot sing?"

"Oh, yes! She told me so herself! She says she carries a tune as well as a mouse can carry a cow. If she really loves me, then she will endure the mortification of singing and embarrass herself."

Kenneth couldn't help but point out the flaw in the plan. "But if you make her embarrass herself publicly, will she not despise you?"

Tisdale shrugged as if he didn't care. "A man likes to know how far a woman will go to earn his fortune."

Truth. *Damn.*

*****

"Sing, my lord? Are you sure?" Evelyn couldn't believe her ears. Lord Tisdale had asked her right in front of three other titled men, as well as the other man she had been introduced to. *What was his name? Mr. Patience? Mr. Non-important? Mr. Odd?*

How could he ask this of her? Lord Tisdale knew she had little talent for it.

Lord Tisdale smiled handsomely and said, "I am afraid it is my dearest wish. Then perhaps we can get some fresh air on the balcony. I have a particular thing I need to discuss with you. Besides, like you my dear, the stars are at their finest tonight."

She didn't mean to hesitate, but to agree to sing was beyond what she was willing to do. She protested, looking at the other expectant faces. A few of them encouraged her to do it, even saying she was being too modest.

But there was something in Mr. Irritating's eyes that was different, almost pity. She squared her shoulders a bit. No one pitied Evelyn Hughes.

Upon meeting her eyes Mr. Silence, or whatever his name was, offered her a way out, which she was sorely tempted to use. "Your voice earlier sounded a bit hoarse. Are you sure it would be wise to sing? You might injure it further."

Lord Tisdale quickly put his hand on Mr. Silence's shoulder and gently guided his person back a few inches. "Nonsense, Silence. Her voice is just as sweet as ever. You were too far down the table to hear it. Not to mention she had lemonade with her meal. I have heard opera singers prepare their voices that way. Come." He took Evelyn's hand and led her to the pianoforte. "Do it for me, my dear." He then kissed her hand.

Somehow—and she was not sure how, for she never truly agreed to it—she found herself seated at the pianoforte.

The room grew silent as Lord Tisdale announced that this would be a performance to remember.

That much is true.

She felt herself grow warm under the scrutiny of those around her. She shuffled the music until she found one that looked easy enough. The second hand only held one or two notes and would be easily read. She realized she had heard it before, too. She thanked God that she barely knew how to sight read simple music, because there was nothing else she knew by heart. It was going to be this or nothing.

She sat down and arranged the papers. Suddenly she heard a calm voice that said, "Allow me to turn your pages." It was Mr. Say-the-worst-possible-thing.

He had a gigantic cigar in his hand and he took a big puff of it and blew it towards her.

How rude!

If anyone was going to turn her pages it should be Lord Tisdale! Who was this Mr. Silence anyway? He certainly wasn't being silent.

From what she could tell, he was better named Mr. Overbearing or Mr. Brash. She thought he did not like her much, because when they were introduced he left after a few short sentences without even bowing farewell. At the time she didn't care, because her attention was on Lord Tisdale. However, looking back, she decided that had been quite arrogant and dismissive! He should be *named* Mr. Dismissive! He didn't even offer the simplest polite compliment to her. Everyone knew that a gentleman must compliment the hair, or the dress, or the jewelry when introduced to a lady.

And here he was, taking the role of suitor by turning her pages.

She had ignored the first puff of smoke in her direction, but the second seemed almost intentional. They both coughed simultaneously, and he then said as quietly as possible, "Are you sure you want to do this? You could claim the cigar smoke is making you cough."

She glared at him. "I must do this. I do not need anyone to turn my pages. Thank you, Mr. Silence."

"Silence," he grumbled.

"Excuse me? Are you truly telling me to be quiet?"

"No, my name is Silence. Calling me Mr. Silence will only make me look around for my late father's ghost. He always did threaten to haunt me."

It almost made her laugh, but her anxiety was already piqued and there was no stopping it from getting worse. Her hands shook and she felt her heart speed up with worry. The guests were all taking their seats. He took another puff of smoke, and this time she was sure he blew it in her face with purpose.

"Will you desist! It is disgusting!" she hissed. "What a filthy habit."

He seemed to ignore her and took another puff of smoke and asked quietly, "How well do you know this song?"

She tried not to groan. Her anxiety was building, and having a stranger sitting next to her irritating her, was unhelpful by half.

He seemed to truly be asking, though, so she answered, "I have heard it before, and it looks easy enough to sight read, but I have no other options. All the other music is too difficult."

Mr. Silence did not say anything for a minute. All the room was staring at her.

She placed her hands on the keys and then Mr. Silence reached his hand, with the cigar still in it, across the last two pages. Hidden from the view of others, he allowed his cigar to light the music on fire.

He stood and shuffled the papers, managing to light the other two papers on fire, too.

There was no denying it, and it was only clear to Evelyn, he had done it with mal intent. She turned her head to his while he pretended to put out the fire.

He glanced her way guiltily. His hazel eyes flinched a bit. He clearly caught the anger she intentionally flashed at him.

While the room erupted in gasps and shouts for water to be brought, she hissed at him, "How could you?"

Silence put the fire out and fumbled a bit, which looked to be all show and no real clumsiness. He looked up to the room and apologized to all the shocked faces. There was a servant who came and started cleaning up the charred paper, but that did not stop her from hissing in his ear again. "Why did you do that? You are an arrogant, interfering fool!"

He looked right into her eyes with a smoldering, somewhat fierce, look that made her breath catch slightly. "I will match your honesty tit for tat. You are a pompous, prideful, entitled, selfish, and ungrateful lady who is blinded by the desire for money and connections. You are welcome."

"I did not say thank you! I most certainly did not!" she countered.

He shrugged and confidently said, "No, you didn't. But you will thank me someday."

CHAPTER 1

Five Months later

Evelyn Hughes closed the Good Book. She had just been reading a powerful verse that made her stop in her tracks. She closed her eyes and repeated the sacred words in her mind.

"And so, after he had patiently endured, he obtained the promise."

It was very fitting of her new circumstances if she just replaced "he" with "she". She felt so enlightened. There was so much hope in this verse. She knew why her circumstances had changed—and she would never go back and do it differently—but it still didn't make it easy.

Reverends and pastors throughout her life had preached from the pulpit, quoting the Bible. For most people, Sunday worship was enough. But not for Evelyn Hughes. It never had been. She went to the scriptures often for her answers. Especially lately.

Ester's sweet voice broke her concentration. "Evie? Are you well? You are crying again."

Evelyn wiped her eyes and smiled at her sister. She looked at her rounded face and stood and hugged her. "No, Ester, everything is just as it should be." She went back to the small table, a table that hardly was big enough for two plates but perfect for her scripture reading. She gingerly took the Bible and opened it back up to Hebrews 6:15.

"I have been praying on how I can help you more than I am—"

But her sister interrupted her. "Evie, how can you say that? There simply is no other possible way you can do more for me than you are."

"Perhaps, and yes, I know you are eternally grateful. But there has to be something I can do. This scripture was the answer to my prayers. Here, read verse fifteen."

Ester read, then started nodding and smiled also. "It is a beautiful verse."

"The first few verses before this one are perfect, too. Verse ten says that God will not forget our work. And verse twelve says that if we are not slothful, and continue with faith and patience, we will inherit the promises. Then in verse fifteen it says, 'After he had patiently endured, he obtained the promise.' That is what God is requiring of us. We have to endure."

"Oh, Evelyn, how can you not regret your decision?"

"Now hear me out, and this time listen. I made my decision and I shall never look back. I felt the rightness of it in my bones. As surely as you know you love Phillip, I know that my place is here with you. Now, if *I* do not feel pity for myself, I shall not let *you* do so in my stead. I am happier than I have ever been. It is true that my life is not perfect. I still miss my friends and society dearly, but no one is more important than family. My place is with you."

She added privately, to herself, *There simply was no other choice.*

*****

Early May in Suffolk was usually wet, foggy, and humid, but the day was hinting at sunshine. Kenneth acknowledged that it was not the best time for his friend, Gavin Kingston, the Duke of Huntsman, to host a house party. But, then again, it wasn't the worst; activities were limited to indoor activities for the most part, which usually meant more intimate conversations.

But the duke's new bride, Grace Iverson Kingston, now Duchess of Huntsman, had patiently endured the season in London at Willsing Manor. Knowing Grace as he did, it was not unexpected to see them take their leave of the city and return to their country estate, Fleetwood Place, that held so many childhood memories for them both.

Grace's childhood home had been the neighboring estate, although much smaller, to the Duke of Huntsman's grand castle, which had been in the family for over three hundred years.

It *was* a grand castle, to be sure. This wasn't the first time Kenneth Silence had been to Fleetwood Place. The estate was just as impressive as when he first came here over five years ago when he was invited by Spencer, Gavin's older brother, who had been killed last year in a carriage accident.

He hated to admit it, but being here brought back memories of Spencer. He had lived the life of an entitled rake, but deep down Kenneth knew things about Spencer that helped him dismiss his hideous behavior. Spencer Kingston flirted with every light skirt, but that did not mean he did not know how to commit. Spencer would have sacrificed his very birthright if it meant helping a friend. He was extremely loyal to Kenneth from the very day he met him.

Kenneth's purpose in life changed the day Spencer approached him at university. It was the end of the second semester when Lord Kingston spoke to him for the first time. Kenneth had been challenged far too many times in his early university days by frauds and mockups, and frankly, he had begun to run out of excuses on how to avoid the fights anymore. At least he knew he had earned himself a respectable position with the students after a year of choosing fisticuffs to defend his honor. Or, more truthfully, to reveal those who had *no* honor.

Yes, calling someone out on his lies was the quickest way to a gentleman's duel if he ever desired it. But after the biweekly conquests over his opponent, few challenged him by the end of his first year at Cambridge. It also helped that his lean body had filled out, but now he was quicker on his feet, and his larger stature brought impressive power.

After an especially challenging fight with Lord Rupert—all because Rupert refused to admit he liked gothic novels—Silence had left Rupert in the dirt, whimpering and begging for it to end. He remembered thinking that those challenges had to end somehow.

That was when Lord Spencer Kingston approached him. He was brought back to that moment.

Kenneth could see everyone was hurriedly leaving the scene. He turned around and saw that one had not.

"How did you know, Silence?" The heir to the dukedom asked Kenneth. Kenneth was plenty aware of who Spencer Kingston was, but had no idea that the man knew who he was.

"How did I know . . . what exactly?" he asked curtly. He had barely caught his breath from the fight, but turned to leave when Spencer called after him.

"That he reads gothic novels." His voice was not accusing at all, but was laced with admiration and respect.

They continued walking away because, not three minutes before, someone had shouted to get Professor Dressel. He had no desire for more discipline.

Spencer asked again, "How did you know he was lying?"

They had rounded the corner of the science building and were safely away from anyone overhearing them. Kenneth turned toward him sharply. "Lord Kingston, why do you want to know?"

Spencer smiled at him. "Because I think you can help me. I have watched you face man after man and hold your own, and it always starts with somehow knowing the truth, some deep secret that they do not want revealed. Tell me. How is it you know when someone is lying?"

He shrugged. "I am not quite sure sometimes. Sometimes it is easy, like when someone's eyebrow pinches just a little, or they clasp their hands tighter, or hold their breath a fraction of a second. Sometimes it is the tone they use, as if they were singing and the note was sharp. It offends me, just like the sharp note would make you want to cover your ears." Kenneth rubbed his head. "It gives me a headache."

"So do you always know when someone is lying?"

When Kenneth didn't answer right away, Spencer added, "Let's test it."

Kenneth raised his eyebrow.

Lord Kingston said, "I have never slept with a woman."

"Lie. You have a reputation. But I did not discern that. I have a cousin who could verify it with facts."

Spencer smiled wickedly. "How about something harder?"

Kenneth Silence nodded. It couldn't hurt to play the game a little. It would probably be fun to call someone out on their lies without having to land someone on their backside when they denied it.

"My middle name is Eugene."

"True."

"Very good; I do not share with anyone. Everyone thinks it is Gene. Perhaps if I say that I have over three thousand pounds at my disposal in my dormitory?"

Silence looked at him with pity. "Can you not at least try?"

"One day I am going to run away to Scotland and give up my title."

There was no falsehood in the words, but it still was not entirely true. "Yes, you are going to run away to Scotland, but you will not give up your title."

Spencer's eyebrows rose dramatically. "Very good! What gave it away?"

"Your voice was quieter with the first part of the declaration, and that meant you hold that part sacred. Deep down, it is the deepest wish of your heart. But then your eyes drifted down to my chest when you said you would give up your title. People have a very hard time looking you in the eye when they lie."

"So you knew which part was true and which part was false? Your talent is better than I thought. See here, I suspect I can help you if you want to avoid these biweekly brawls in the courtyard."

What he said rang true. He was not lying. Well, at least Spencer believed his own declaration.

That was enough to make Kenneth curious. "How?"

"You are a third son, correct? And you have to have a profession, since you will most likely not inherit anything. Is that accurate?"

"Accurate on both accounts. I have to work for a living, which is why I must study law."

"Then perhaps from now on, I will help you. You will find that this talent for knowing when someone lies will make you the most successful lawman there ever was. Delinquents will flinch at your name alone. This talent you have, it cannot be wasted. But it is much more powerful than your fists."

From that day on, Silence's life changed. He learned from Spencer when to hold his tongue, to allow a lie to pass him and not crucify the offender. He learned that an aggressive confrontation only made people distrust you and shut down, therefore adding to the lie even more. He learned to tame his talent for truth seeking, and not offend those with the greatest influence in the world by calling them out every few weeks.

In short, he learned to be charming. Spencer taught him that a true gentleman finds a way to not only communicate the truth but learn the truth as well, through being silent and charming.

In a way, he learned to live up to his name.

Slowly, over the next three years of university, Spencer and Kenneth became incredibly close. Silence's fist year of brawling had earned him a respect that could not be bought. Being the next Duke of Huntsman's closest friend opened doors to many opportunities in society as well. Spencer was, in fact, the one who introduced him to most of his acquaintances and, as he rubbed shoulders with other powerful men, he earned their respect. Men trusted him so much that he became their confidant, and they asked him to help them with one thing or another.

Once, a jealous husband asked him to identify the person his wife was sleeping with. There was no formal agreement for payment, but when Silence came to him with the information that his wife appeared completely faithful to him suddenly Kenneth's butler's annual salary was paid up in full.

Word started spreading. An associate he hardly knew asked him to investigate which of his servants had a loose tongue and was spreading family secrets. When he found out who it was, the servant was dismissed from the household, and Silence's tailor's bill was miraculously paid, with a credit of 300 pounds to use later.

Odd jobs became rather frequent, and Silence started working out payment plans before accepting a job. He got rather efficient at predicting how much a job would cost. Most of the time the agreement was that Kenneth would keep track of the time it took, and his expenses for travel or other costs, like meals, and he would send the customer updates as he went along. Very few jobs went over budget, but nearly every customer was so pleased with his quick work that bonuses were given in other ways.

One father was so happy with how the search turned out that he practically offered marriage to his only daughter, an heiress with a fifteen-thousand-pound dowry. That was when Silence really understood the power of his talent for detecting falsehoods. He couldn't afford not to "investigate" his chance at marrying an heiress, but it turned out the man's daughter was rather brash and had putrid breath. He couldn't imagine kissing her, and therefore he politely declined the father's offer.

But sometimes jobs just landed on his doorstep. About a year ago, his friend Spencer was accused of compromising the Earl of Longmont's daughter. It was very clear to Kenneth, when Spencer denied it, that Spencer was telling the truth. Before Kenneth had a chance to offer his services and find out who really did compromise the earl's daughter, the duel was set and the horrible accident occurred where Spencer's father, the Duke of Huntsman, was shot, and Spencer, in a crazed panic, went chasing after the earl who had shot him.

Silence had been there in the misty meadow the morning when the Earl of Longmont's gun went off. He had also been the first one on the scene when he found Spencer's carriage turned over about a mile down the road. Spencer was severely injured, and Kenneth never got a chance to sufficiently thank him for teaching him how to use his talent all those years ago at Cambridge.

Kenneth Silence stayed by his friend's side until he took his last breath, less than twenty- four hours after the duel.

The Earl of Longmont went into hiding, and Kenneth vowed to find him. With both Spencer and his father dead, Gavin, the younger brother, found himself being called back from the navy to take the title. Silence had known Gavin fairly well, but he soon became one of his closest confidants because of Kenneth's usefulness as an investigator. Gavin didn't even have to ask. It took six months, but when the case closed last October in a crazy, convoluted two days, no money needed to be exchanged. Of course Gavin tried to pay him, and Silence refused.

He did it for his friend, Spencer.

But what he wasn't expecting with Spencer's death was how close he would become with Gavin. He had learned to respect him and trust him more than any other person. He was a true gentleman, and it was clear that his devotion to his wife was unparalleled.

That was why he could not, in good conscience, refuse to attend the house party at Gavin's country estate in Suffolk. Silence knew it was to introduce him to ladies that the duke and duchess felt were eligible.

He decided that a philosopher would enjoy an hour pondering why it was that a married man, who once vowed to never marry, felt the insatiable need to "help" others find the same giddy abandon.

No, he could not refuse to come to the house party, but neither did he have to force love with any of the ladies either. Silence was nine and twenty, had a solid profession and income using his tamed talent. There was no reason he needed to rush into an understanding with some chit just because she was eligible.

Kenneth knew that coming to Fleetwood Place two weeks ago meant a great deal of his spare time would be spent entertaining these ladies, but he found his spare time was with Gavin.

It was a good bet that where Gavin was, so was Grace. The newly married, moonstruck lovebirds were inseparable. They could hardly be in the same room without being at each other's side or communicating sweet nothings from across the room.

But a single gentleman can only take so much fawning and witness so many stolen kisses without feeling the ache of loneliness. The house party would come to an end in less than a week, and Gavin had failed to find him the perfect match.

Months ago, Kenneth realized that he appreciated beauty. He found quite a bit of enjoyment in flirting with certain ladies—

the ladies who were never flirted with. But he couldn't deny that there was something missing in these meaningless flirtations.

The harder he tried to find "the one", the more he became increasingly blind finding her. At the moment he felt like he was in a thick fog as eligible ladies' skirts brushed past him suggestively on their way to break their fast.

He sighed and caught the duchess looking at him sympathetically.

When their eyes met she smiled and then whispered to her husband, who also looked at Kenneth.

The duke bid a few of the ladies good morning as he made his way through the breakfast parlor of Fleetwood Place.

Kenneth knew that look. He obediently followed the Duke of Huntsman into his study.

If asked about it later, he would have reported that they had talked for a few minutes. However, he doubted he would be able to recall anything, regardless of his instinctual attention to detail.

Gavin's brows were slightly pinched. "You are entirely too silent these last few days. You have not been yourself."

Kenneth chuckled a little at the silliness of his favorite game. "So you are saying that I, Silence, am too silent and not being myself. How ironic."

Gavin gave a polite laugh, but it was clear that he would not be dissuaded. "You do not seem as if you have a particular preference for any of the ladies. What about Miss Pardee? She is fetching."

"Yes, but fetching is not the only trick she knows. She has no opinions, and waits for me to tell her what to do. I bet if I said 'sit' she would sit. Then if I asked her to roll over she would not hesitate. She has nothing that distinguishes her as an individual."

"You want someone more opinionated?"

"Well, I want someone who is passionate about something. Someone who is willing to drive the conversation. I get tired of the meaningless prattle."

"Then why not Miss Hadlock?"

"Jane?"

Gavin smiled. "You are on a first-name basis with her?"

Kenneth chuckled. "Do not forget that I worked with her father. I saw her change from a wee girl into the young lady she is now. Yes, Jane Hadlock is a sweet young lady who offers good conversation, but she is not what I am looking for. At least I do not think so. I do have to admit that her eyes are about the finest I have ever seen. I find myself looking at them, trying to decide what color they are. I swear to you they change color. Sometimes they are green, other times they have so much yellow in them that they are nearly golden. Then other times, when she is tired, they are grey blue. She is beyond beautiful, but too quiet. I will concede, she does not seem to present false fronts like Miss Macy."

Gavin looked at him curiously. "Grace and I hoped you would be attracted to one of these ladies. If you need more time with Miss Hadlock, I can suggest to her father that she stay longer."

Kenneth paused a minute before answering. It was true that, of all the ladies at the house party, Miss Hadlock was the most intriguing. "I cannot explain it to you, Kingston. Somewhere, there is the right woman for me. She will be smart, quick-witted, and have a genuine heart. It has been several months, nearly half a year, since I started losing my desire to flirt with any pretty skirt. I suppose I am tired of the games. I want someone who speaks the truth without hesitation. You know my reasons for that. Maybe then my headache will go away for good."

Concern crossed his friend's features. "Do the powders not help?"

"Oh, they help, but the headache is not a physical ache. It stems from the tension that invades with every social attraction where people pretend to be someone they are not. It is nearly constant. Miss Hadlock does make it better, yet because I have made no decision to pursue her I have been hesitant to show preference. I do not usually have this trouble making up my mind."

"When you are troubled, what do you do?"

Kenneth knew the answer. "I ride. I ride for hours."

"Well, then, I suggest you ride. I can make your excuses at breakfast. Miss Macy will surely take note of your absence, and I will let them know that you had some business to attend to."

"Thanks, Kingston. It might be just the thing I need to find what I am lacking."

CHAPTER 2

Evelyn had a great deal to do before the noon meal, but none of it sounded appealing. She chose instead to pick up her intriguing book that was near to rounding the climactic moment.

Unfortunately, their friend's—and now their only servant's—words from last night came ringing in her ears: *"Lose an hour in the mornin' and you'll be looking for it all day."*

Guilt bade her to put her book down, and she did so with some frustration, earning a look from Ester, which she ignored.

"I should probably go into town and get the ingredients we need for the stew Mrs. Farnsworth will be showing us how to make tonight. Do you remember if she said to get venison or a ham hock?"

Ester scrunched up her face and said, "I believe she said venison, but do you think we could make it with a ham hock instead? I cannot say I am all that fond of game meat lately. Not after the rabbit that tasted, well, colorful."

She giggled a little. "Let us hope it was a ham hock."

Evelyn finished buttoning her pelisse, filled her arms with empty baskets and snatched her bonnet off the single-nail peg, and went out the front door of the cottage. The door creaked as much as ever.

Honeymae greeted her with a slobbery lick on her hand, which she returned with a tousle of her fur. She was grateful her parents allowed her to have her dog when they were sent to live in this small cottage.

She saw Eddie, their only servant, working with a hoe at the ground like it was the only thing that could buy him happiness. She waved at him and walked towards him.

Eddie Malloy was probably in his early forties and had greying hair at the temples. He always wore a farmer's hat, even indoors, with a broad rim that no longer held its shape or did much more than shield the sun, when forced. It always made him look taller than he was, which was nearly as tall as Lord Tisdale. She had probably only ever seen more than four or five men who were as tall as Eddie.

His partly open shirt billowed in the breeze, enough to hint at how well built he was.

She worked to untie the bonnet ribbons as she neared him. He smiled at her with a warm, fatherly smile, his slightly crooked teeth making their appearance. He stopped hoeing and leaned against the tool.

Touching his hat briefly, he said in his Irish brogue, "I see ye won't be a lookin' for that hour all day like I warned ya 'bout."

"Yes, and I should thank you for your wisdom. Although I would much rather read my book! How are you this morning?"

"Mighty good, thank you kindly. This garden was callin' me name and thought middle of May was creeping up rather fast and all. We best be plantin' the summer vegetables. What say you? If you are goin' to town, might you find some seed for it?"

"I was thinking the same thing yesterday."

"Me ma always says that 'You never plow a field by turnin' it over in yer head.'"

"You know what I think, Eddie? Your Irish accent gets rather thick when you quote your mother."

She smiled at him and then focused her attention back on the ribbons of her bonnet. It had an especially tight knot.

"Aye. I suspect it does. Thank you kindly. That is how you know I'm tellin' the truth! When I have to think about what I say my brogue is diluted, but when I spout off the first thing that comes to me mind it is as thick and pure as the honey from me pa's beehive back home. Now, off with ya. I suspect it will be some time before I see the likes of you."

"Yes, I will be walking today. As usual."

"Wish I could help, Miss Hughes."

"I know you do."

She tried hard not to display her frustration with the bonnet, but it must have shown because he pulled the knife from his boot, offered it to her, and said, "If it offends thee, smite it with a sword."

She giggled. "No, thank you. I rather like this bonnet and do not wish to add it to my mending. Sheath that blade. Ah, see? It just took a bit of patience and work." She placed her bonnet on her head and headed towards town.

*****

It was a bruising few hours of riding, but it had been worth it. Kenneth Silence could feel the anxiety drip from him with each jump and landing that Nimbus performed flawlessly. Nimbus was the best horse he had ever owned and could read the subtlest of commands, from the knee pressed to his side to the change of pressure in his seat. Nimbus enjoyed these rides, perhaps more than Kenneth did. But he could see the lathered sweat on his shoulders and hear his horse's labored breathing.

One more jump, and I'll pull up on the reins, he told himself. He leaned forward, seeing the perfect fence ahead of him.

He pressed his heels in more and let out a holler, "One more, Nimbus!"

As he expected, Nimbus' hooves acknowledged the command and clods of dirt flung from beneath them, making the thundering sound that stirred Kenneth. At breakneck speed, he approached the hill ahead. At this speed, the ride was as smooth as running your hand on polished marble. Nimbus was fluid and powerful in his movements, but no less confident than he that the upcoming jump would be a favorite.

If he had any luck, the fence that he was aiming for would have a bit of a drop since it crested the hill at precisely the right angle. He leaned forward in preparation and could tell Nimbus was anticipating it, too.

Drat! A bonnet! A bonnet?

It is strange how one can make spur of the moment decisions in a fraction of the time it would take to process the various scenarios that run through one's mind.

When he saw the blasted blue bonnet, there were only two choices to make: either pull up on the reins and be thrown, or steer to the side and hope to miss her.

At this speed both were very risky, and both were likely to have poor outcomes. Either for her, him, or both.

He chose to pull up on the reins.

Of course he flew headfirst, then shoulders over the horse, and finally his heels cleared Nimbus' head. He had no time to change the torque of how he would land, but he had a perfect view of the wretched bonnet-wearing female as his body finished the inverted arch.

The swear word may have slipped out of habit, but the cavernous ache coming from his tailbone also could have knocked the word right out of him, along with what he feared was his last breath.

He was vaguely aware there was a woman, whom he had already deemed, "Miss Bonnet", for there was more bonnet than lady, stooping and asking how he was.

He shook the feeling of confusion from his head. It took doing it a second time before he was sure he wasn't going to pass out.

Slowly, the vise on his chest let loose enough to pull in a quarter of the breath he desired. He tried again and felt some relief with the second breath. As he sat there on his backside, legs out in front of him, he felt the cool wet puddle that he had fallen into seep into his breeches.

With herculean effort, he rolled to his hands and knees and crawled out of the puddle. In doing so, he found his limbs were cooperative and functional. "Tender mercy, for sure," he muttered, surprised that his breath was still hitched.

"Sir? Are you well? That was quite the spill."

"My horse . . ." he croaked out.

"He is obediently waiting. Are you injured?"

He took another deep breath and felt true relief, as it no longer felt like one of those afternoons on the courtyard at Cambridge. He took another breath or two and inventoried his other aches. Besides a tender tailbone, he was intact. He made an attempt to stand as pain shot through his hip momentarily, but it was nothing he couldn't push through.

"Can I help in some way? Perhaps you should not get up quite yet."

Now that Kenneth could breathe again, he looked at Miss Bonnet. Her dress was finer than a farmer's daughter, but she certainly wasn't a lady. Her hideous bonnet, full of more silk flowers, ribbons and feathers, was low over her eyes, making it hard to see her face, especially since the sun was right behind her.

He cleared his throat, which brought some strength to it. "I think I shall be fine. Just humbled a bit. It is not often I land in a puddle at the foot of a woman. Will you help me up? My name is Silence."

The woman had been reaching towards him to do just that, and then she stopped, dropped the arm she had been extending, and stood up.

Miss Bonnet very pointedly hissed, "You are welcome."

"It is not often that I get confused. I definitely did not say thank you."

"No, but *you will thank me someday.*"

The way she said the last sentence was supposed to mean something, but he could not fathom what.

Her entire demeanor changed from tender and solicitous to cool and dismissive. If that blasted sun was not right behind her he might be able to see her facial expressions.

"Very well, I was only allowing you to help me since you offered to help." He wasn't sure what had changed, but he pulled himself up to one knee and then paused. The sharp pain he felt in the movement made him flinch slightly, but he pressed through until he was standing.

Only then did he recognize who Miss Bonnet was. "Miss Hughes—"

"Mr. Silence," she said curtly. Her eyes flashed a fiery mixture of anger and pain. She was restraining herself for sure.

There was a prolonged moment when neither of them spoke, but rather just stared at each other. Finally, she bent down and started picking up the vegetables she must have dropped and put them in her two oversized baskets. It was his instinct, as a gentleman, to reach and pick up the rest of the vegetables, but each time he bent over the pain shot through his tailbone all the way down to his toes. A small moan escaped the first time it happened, but he continued to pick up the vegetables. He tried to hide the pain, but it was not easy.

Miss Hughes stood up and took the last vegetable from Kenneth's hand. "I thank you. However, let me say this plainly: I do not ever want your help again."

Her words had a finality to them.

*****

"You cannot still be mad about the music at the Halliburtons' dinner party."

Evelyn had already turned away and continued walking away. She heard him grunt a little but she was not going to spend one more minute with him.

She adjusted the heavy baskets and started the decent down the hill.

"Heaven help me, Miss Hughes. Wait. Let me take those baskets. They look heavy."

She turned around to see that he was leading his horse toward her with a stiff, awkward gait, as if he was still in pain.

"I believe I said I do not need your help now, nor ever!"

"I cannot just leave a lady carrying ten kilos of produce! What kind of gentleman would I be?"

"No kind of gentleman at all! But that should feel natural to you." She turned forward again and picked up her pace.

If he wouldn't listen, let him and his horse hobble toward her at a faster pace. Then he might give up. They walked behind her and slowly she could hear his gait become more even and hurried.

"Are you calling me ungentlemanly?"

"How are your shoes fitting?" she called out, proud that she could think of the retort so quickly.

"Oh, ill-humored, are we? By the way, the saying is: 'If the shoe fits.'"

She chose not to acknowledge his comment and continued walking. The baskets were very heavy, and she felt the handles pressing into her forearms. The ache in her shoulders from carrying them all the way from town was building. She truly only had the better part of a mile left.

Somehow he caught up, even with her quick pace. He continued to chatter a bit as they progressed, telling her about the house party at Fleetwood Place with the Duke of Huntsman. He told her about how long he had been out riding, three hours apparently, and how he was just going to do one more jump before heading back, when he was thrown.

He even introduced her to his horse, Nimbus.

Who names their horse Nimbus? Didn't that mean "a halo surrounding a supernatural being or saint"? He was quite arrogant if he thought he was a saint. Perhaps somewhere in time the Greeks had incorrectly transcribed the age-old myth, and Nimbus didn't surround a saint but rather a devil.

He persisted talking while they walked. The man was persistent. Even though she willed herself not to, she stole a glance in his direction. He was still limping a bit, his back slightly arched as if leaning over was painful.

She stopped and looked at him. "What do you want, Mr. Silence?"

"Silence. It is what I want, but never receive." He seemed to laugh at his own joke a bit. "Sorry. My name is Silence, just Silence."

"It does not seem to fit you."

"That is what everyone says. But alas, it is my name. I simply prefer it to be Silence, with no 'Mister' in front of it. Makes people adore me more."

She scoffed and his eyebrows rose.

She didn't mean to be so rude, but she had her own opinion about him, and whether or not she used 'Mister' in front of his name had nothing to do with it.

Before she could restrain herself, she told him exactly that.

He smiled at her, and then had the gall to wink!

"You have caused me to be thrown from my horse, refused to assist me, called me ungentlemanly, and somehow you think I should be surprised that you do *not* like me?"

"Well, it is true. I do not like you one bit."

"Yes, I know." He smiled further. "It is rather refreshing."

"Pardon me? Oh, I see. It must be so common that all the ladies fall at your feet, adoring your handsome looks and strong shoulders and unparalleled wit. I must be the exception."

Silence chuckled a little, and then started laughing in earnest. "Handsome? Unparalleled wit? If I did not know better, I would say you were lying to me about not liking me."

"I think you *are* arrogant!"

"Now, *that* I believe."

He was talking circles around her and loving it! It made her anger rise to new levels. "What is that supposed to mean?"

"Indeed, nothing. I just know that is exactly how you *truly* feel. But this is how *I* truly feel—"

With quick work, he had taken the heaviest basket and motioned with his other hand to lead the way.

The physical relief of having that weight off her arm was simply not quantifiable.

Evelyn was at a point where she had to make a decision. They were nearly in sight of the cottage, and he had the basket with the ham hock in it for tonight's stew. Either she should let him have the basket, or she would lead him right to where she and Ester were living in their reduced circumstances.

She had promised to keep it intimately secret.

Not even her dearest friends knew where she was.

She didn't know what rumors were circulating about her. All her letters were posted through another person, and those that came to her parents' house in London were forwarded to her the same way. How could she let a total stranger in on the secret, when she did not even tell her best friends, Lydia and Maria, who had stood by her since she was twelve years old?

Time seemed to pause for a little as she focused her mind for an extended second.

Silence made the decision for her. "Since I know you are not at the duke's house party, I am going to assume you live around here. We have gone down a hill, followed the river to the west for half a mile, and yet the next three miles of travel are still on Kingston property. Unless you plan to cut across the cavern, then it might be a third of the distance. Have the duke and duchess built a bridge I do not know about? No, they have not. So I am assuming that the duke knows you are staying here, on his land. I am his closest friend, you can tell me."

She closed her eyes for a moment.

She sighed. She was not free to make any other decision. "Please. Grant me my baskets. I can journey from here. I am not unaware that you are still hurting from being thrown. If you are any kind of gentleman, please take your leave." She didn't mean to sound desperate, but she was, and it was hard not to have it trickle into her tone.

He studied her for a minute and then handed her the basket and bowed. She watched him mount his horse and turn, trotting the other direction.

For a brief moment, she missed the companionship. She hadn't talked to anyone for months besides Ester, Eddie, and the cook who came once a week, Mrs. Farnsworth. Her eyes pricked with the sting of tears.

It was a very challenging thing to carry two heavy burdens and not have your hands free to wipe your eyes.

BUYING THE DUKE'S SILENCE

CHAPTER 3

Usually Ester and Evelyn shared everything. But Evelyn would not share what happened next with her sister.

She did not want her to know how she had watched Silence charge over the hill, and then how she collapsed on the grass in tears.

She was so tired, and the interaction with Silence deeply troubled her. She hadn't thought about the Halliburtons' dinner for many months. In fact, she had exerted great effort to keep herself from thinking of Lord Tisdale.

Over and over again she had repressed, and carefully folded, all those painful memories and tucked them away. Little by little she had learned to keep her head high in the face of the change, all the while pushing those folded feelings deeper and deeper inside.

Her heart was, in truth, a most tender one, but pain was a humble teacher. It taught her to face things with strength and coolness. It taught her that when the cart was in the mud, the only way through was to push it out, with your shoulder to the wheel.

Crying just did not help. But *not* crying simply wasn't natural.

She used to be a very emotional person. But her emotional barricade had saved her time and time again. It had been many weeks since she'd broken down like this. Her wall must have given her a false sense of security. Today, Silence had knocked down those barriers.

As she lay weeping in the grass, she tried to build the wall back up again.

One brick was to not feel the pain of those dinner party guests' judging eyes. Another was to forget the intrigued smile on

Lord Tisdale's face that forgave her, almost immediately, for failing to fulfill his wish for her to sing.

That thought brought on more bricks, the loss of the possibility of love. Would she and Lord Tisdale have been married by now? Another brick in the wall was channeling her anger towards her parents for what happened the day after the Halliburtons' dinner.

Several more bricks were placed almost daily, as she learned to do the hard labor required of her in the circumstances she was now in.

And as much as she adored society, an entire row of bricks was added as she recommitted to refusing to feel the absence of her closest friends. She missed the soirees, the balls, Almack's. All of it.

She was the kind of person who thrived on and found great meaning in her relationships. Her sister and friends were her closest confidantes, and she felt revived after being with them.

Being isolated as she was was truly a challenge. It wasn't that she regretted her decision; she didn't. It was that she hoped to help her sister *and* have her friends. But she couldn't have her cake and chew it, too. *Was that the right saying?* It felt wrong, but she could not think of any other way to say it.

Her heart ached for the tenderness that she felt from the gentlemen she danced with. She knew many people did not enjoy paying calls on people, but Evelyn loved it all.

So right there on the grass, as she watched the only gentleman she had conversed with in months, ride off without even a glance back at her, she found she was heartbroken.

Was she really so starved for notice that she would welcome the attentions of a rude, arrogant man like Silence?

Sadly, she was.

All the bricks that she had built over the last five months started crumbling down again around her. How had her life come to this?

In that moment, she felt all the loneliness the last five months had brought.

She felt all the soreness her parents had imposed upon her.

She felt the calluses on her hands as she dabbed at her tears.

She felt the fatigue in her bones.

And she cried.

*****

By the time she had regained composure the sun was growing deep orange on the horizon, and that meant that she needed to return and meet Mrs. Farnsworth. She collected herself and lifted the heavy baskets, walking around the large oak tree, the one that held the rope swing that she loved so much.

She had no time for herself lately, but when she did she usually chose to swing under that grand canopy of leaves.

It looked like Eddie was putting the tools away. When he saw her, he hustled up the hill and met her halfway and took the baskets.

He whistled when he saw the full baskets. "My oh my, did ye spend all the allowance yer father sent?"

"Of course not, Eddie; you know there is no end to what my father will pay for. It is the one thing I am grateful for."

He fished through the baskets, no doubt looking for the seed she bought.

He then challenged her, without looking her in the eye. "He won't give ye a maid. Or a cook."

She unconsciously sighed, which of course brought Eddie's attention away from the baskets and up to her face.

She quickly averted her eyes. She had no idea how much evidence there was of the sobbing she had just done. Choosing not to answer him gave her great satisfaction because they had had this conversation before.

He knew her father felt that they needed to feel the discomfort entirely, rather than live in the country with ease. She remembered his words in his last letter. *"Maybe then your decisions will begin to reflect the ladies society should see."*

But instead of a lecture, Eddie tried to lighten the situation. She was grateful he came up with one of his dictums from Ireland. "'Tis better to spend money like there is no tomorrow than spend today like there is no money."

She giggled. "And that is supposed to be wise?"

"I've never said Irish dictums were wise. They jus' make ye think."

"How is that supposed to make me think?"

"Well, missy, it means to revel in the joy today brings. Recognize the moment yer in and really live in it. Buy yer souvenir and remember today always. Don't be a waiting on yer ship to come sailin' in tomorrow. Don't be a'saying, 'someday I'll enjoy myself.' Make today count. Even if 'tis hard, there'll be ways to appreciate it. Am I right, Miss Evelyn?"

"You are always right, Eddie. I need to appreciate today."

"That's why they be callin' it the present. Seein' as you know that now, me job is complete. I best be washing off the tools. Miss Ester received another one of her missives." He motioned with his head toward the cottage. "She is anxious to talk to ya."

"Oh, splendid!"

She took the baskets from him and went inside. Ester was already at the little table, writing her response.

"Another letter from Phillip?"

Ester looked up and smiled sweetly. "He made it to Falmouth. He has been asking around for work. He met several people who gave him a day's worth of work, but nothing permanent. He has a lead that might allow him a month of sailing. He will write more when he knows."

Evelyn smiled mischievously. She nonchalantly walked toward the small table, snatched the letter, and held it high above her head when Ester reached for it.

Ester awkwardly stood and futilely reached for the letter. "Evelyn! Give it back!"

Evelyn backed away from her sister. "Oh, I am sure you told me everything that was in the letter from your 'dear sweet man!' I am sure the letter had nothing but facts about his prospects in employment. I am sure that the urgency you feel in replying back has nothing to do with the fact that he said . . ." she looked up at the letter and read, "'A man's heart can burst from aching to hold his lady, this much I am sure. I hold your letters every night. I smell the pressed paper, hoping that I can recall how lovely you smelled in the fall as we ate our pasties from the café at Piccadilly Circus. I remember that night well. It was the first night you let me-—'"

"Stop! Evelyn, give me back the letter!"

She giggled and handed back the letter. "I do not know why you do not just let me read the whole thing."

"There are some secrets that I like to keep to myself."

"Do not forget, Ester, that I know exactly what happened at Piccadilly Circus. You could not stop flushing scarlet every time we drove by! I believe one time you even closed your eyes and leaned back in the carriage and imagined your first kiss all over again!"

Ester blushed and said, "You know what? Sometimes having a sister like you can be very trying! You read me too well!"

Evelyn nodded in agreement. "It comes with the territory. Remember, you may be the eldest, but that does not make you wiser. Now, tell me more. You know his letters are the highlight of our week."

They both sat down and Ester said, "Well, he is hoping the voyage he might be going on will be the answer we are looking for. Apparently the shipman who told him about the job says the captain needs a first mate. A second in charge, someone he can train to take over when he retires next year. You know Thomas served in the navy a few years back, but there has been no real way to earn his keep with peace upon us."

"And we do not wish war to resume just so he has work!"

"Exactly. But this job will be managing shipments fairly regularly from London to Falmouth. One month at a time at sea, with two weeks off between shipments. He is not sure of how much it will pay as a shipman, but if he were to be the apprentice for the captain the possibility of advancement within a year is very likely!"

"But Ester, how can you be married to a man who is gone for a month at a time?"

Her sister looked down at her hands, and the hope in her voice faded. "It would be better than not having him here at all."

Evelyn suddenly felt very selfish for her moment of self-pity up on the hill behind the ancient oak when Silence left.

Ester loved Phillip so much. Their futures were intertwined. They belonged together. She recommitted herself to serving Ester in anyway possible instead of mourning over her nonexistent life in society's spotlight.

Ester's eyes glossed over. Her pain ran deeper than Evelyn's.

"You know he would be here if he could."

With that, Ester folded up the letter and tucked it into the fishing basket at the foot of her bed with all the other letters they had received over the last five months.

Evelyn stood and hugged her sister, and repeated, "He *would* be here if he could."

*****

It was a full two days before Kenneth could walk without pain. In that time he made use of his time getting to know Jane Hadlock. He wasn't up for much more than talking with her, and the days had been dreadfully rainy anyhow. The more time he spent with her the more he recognized that she was a dear, sweet girl. She was definitely someone he wanted to get to know.

He found himself distracted while conversing with her, though.

Miss Hadlock had three scattered freckles on the bridge of her nose, otherwise she would have had a flawless complexion.

That only made him think of how the sun had brought out Miss Hughes' many intriguing freckles. She possessed significantly more freckles yesterday than five months prior, at the dinner party.

He reminded himself that he had once thought that they were "charming freckles", but had learned of what was the stronger memory that she was actually as bristly as a porcupine.

He put a bit more effort into courting Miss Hadlock.

But the success of that was demonstrated with him sitting still long enough while she talked about—well, he didn't rightly know what Miss Hadlock was talking about—to notice that there were three indistinguishable pillars in the sitting room.

The pillars were identically sculpted, with a chiseled star at the base and mint green and navy blue ring accents. The color pattern occurred three times on the identical pillars.

Silence couldn't see the third pillar's uppermost decorations—the one that was closest to the fireplace—but he assumed it had a crescent moon at the junction of the ceiling, just as the other two.

The sitting room garnered an enormous amount of study. But soon one pillar looked like all the others. Just like one lady looked like all the rest, even Jane Hadlock.

To be true to facts, the days, moments of attempted diversion, and meals went by quickly, but not the nights. Too many were shared with an intruder.

The morning Silence woke up from the first dream, a dream consisting of a mass of strawberry-blonde hair bathing his bare body, he knew he had to do something more than just be in the presence of other ladies to shake her from his thoughts.

He needed to tell her just what he felt.

If she could call him "ungentlemanly", then it broke no social rules for him to return the "compliment".

He would simply tell her—yes, he would—he would simply tell her she had no place invading his dreams! Miss Evelyn Hughes had no consideration for his privacy!

That thought brought him a hearty chuckle. He couldn't imagine being *that* truthful!

Maybe there is a time and place for a lie. That brought on more chuckles, based on the strange look from Miss Hadlock's face, which may not have been appropriately timed.

Thank goodness it appeared time to retire.

The day had begun and ended with rain.

When the third day finally promised sun, he realized that the investigator in him was slightly less distracted by the "who" he had interacted with three days prior than the "why".

Why was Miss Hughes on the duke's land? Why was she not dressing to her station? Why was she in a position to need to carry her own market purchases? Why had pain filled her eyes when he asked if the Duke of Huntington knew she was on his land?

And why, when he crested the hill to leave her as requested, did he have the insatiable urge to turn back and assist?

Was it her honesty? It was quite invigorating not to have a lady lie to him. He had no headache at all when he thought of their interactions.

Was it her fiery pale blue-green eyes that turned bluer as the anger built when she affronted him?

Was it the refreshing way she did not throw herself at him like so many others?

Was it that she had once been someone—who'd been knocked from the aristocratic thrown—yet she still held her head high and proud? He could not answer any of these questions. And that was more disturbing than he expected.

The unanswered questions led him back to Nimbus late in the afternoon on the third day, when he simply *had* to have answers. He knew where in the general vicinity she must be staying.

He told himself he just wanted answers.

He was an information gatherer.

It was his job as an investigator.

She could be in trouble. It was his duty as a gentleman.

Yes, it was.

He tried to suppress the voice telling him no one had hired him to search her out, but it nagged at his conscience anyway.

It took a few minutes for Kenneth Silence to saddle his horse due to residual pain from being thrown over "Miss Bonnet" three days ago. As he bent over to tighten the chest buckles, he reminded himself that he had all afternoon to find Miss Hughes.

His muscles could perform these functions without thinking but, sadly, that meant his thoughts would not submit to anything other than Miss Hughes.

He doubted she would welcome him openly after calling him ungentlemanly.

His brows knit together momentarily, until he consciously corrected them and mounted.

I am worried for *her person, not* because *of her actual person . . . Right?*

He took off in a gallop to try to sort things out in his head, ignoring the moan from his bruised tailbone.

Nimbus slowed prematurely, likely sensing the subtle hesitancy in his rider.

What did he hope to achieve in seeking her out?

He didn't care one bit what happened to that selfish, pompous, and entitled chit. He prodded his horse again and tossed the leads a bit too hard.

He glanced to the left, examining the deep cavern. Nimbus, too, seemed interested. He was more interested in the fact that she was a lady by birth but, currently, not in circumstance. His brow furrowed again without permission.

Months ago he had decided he knew all he cared to know about her, when he overheard her scheming to obtain an offer from Lord Tisdale.

But pride was warranted, now more than ever—and yet she unnaturally repressed it. She did not appear proud anymore. She was different. More natural.

"Other way, Nimbus," he grunted, more to himself than the horse.

She most definitely was a mercenary, spoiled brat who got anything she wanted. People like that never change.

But how could she want her changed circumstances which, if measured, was negligible at best.

"Nimbus, you seem to be confused, too." He redirected his horse up the hill ahead of him, recounting all he knew. Ending with a sum of nothing, and a jumble of parts.

Ungrateful, for sure, to blatantly and unmistakably refuse his help.

His honor was at stake! Honor as a gentleman and a trained professional.

However, something in her pained expression three days ago told him she didn't want the circumstances she was currently in. As if *her* honor was at stake.

He couldn't help it. He couldn't *not* help in some way.

It was in his nature.

And he was going to help her even though she was all of the above, wrapped up in a very pretty redheaded package. Ridiculously fobbed out with a blue, yellow-ribboned bonnet that he despised.

He neared the area he had last seen her. The wind was blowing softly and he heard the song of a meadow pipit.

He slowed his pace and started looking around for where Miss Hughes might call home.

The bird called again, charmingly. Unknowingly, he followed the sound.

Some might say the meadow pipit's dark brown wings made it look plain, like any other bird, but he knew the song of the meadow pipit was unique. Its repeated chirp sounded like a distant echo as it faded into the shadows of the giant oak tree that he had left Miss Hughes at. He paused and listened for a minute, just soaking up the sun and the sounds of late spring.

He then heard a different kind of sound. He heard the sound of a woman laughing.

It wasn't the kind of laughter you hear in town—the forced, polite tones where the woman covers her lips with her fingers. Nor was it the vulgar sound of an uneducated lady who knew not how to behave.

It was the unabashed joy of a lady who was fully enjoying herself.

He knew it was Miss Hughes.

He nudged Nimbus a bit, but he clearly sensed where his master was asking him to go.

Sure enough, Miss Hughes was playing with an enormous brindle-colored English Mastiff. The grey and fawn striped colors, with its semi-wavy pattern, made the canine beast look akin to a tiger. She was clearly enjoying a playful tug-of-war with the dog, and losing quite terribly. The dog would pull her one way, then change directions, forcing her to nearly lose her footing, but it did not trouble her at all.

The joy on her face was innocent and unmasked. It was genuine and endearing. No one watching the game could deny that she adored her dog. He did not know how long he watched them play. It could have only been a few minutes, but certainly not more than a quarter of an hour. The beast growled a bit playfully, but then the young lady let go of the rope. The dog shook the rope triumphantly then brought it back to Miss Hughes.

He could faintly hear her say, "Drop it." And the dog did so immediately. Miss Hughes picked up the knotted rope and threw it, a distance that rather impressed Kenneth. The knotted rope landed in a patch of trees to the side of him and he ducked behind the oak again. The dog thundered towards him, its paws sounding like horse hooves pounding up clods of dirt.

He peeked around the tree at the dog. From this distance, he could tell it was a female.

Kenneth watched as the dog slowed and stuck her nose in the air. She then dropped her head below her shoulders and growled in Kenneth's direction. The growl was low and came from deep inside that massive chest. It moved forward, clearly putting herself more directly between her owner and Silence.

Protective was not adequate to describe the stance the dog took as it slowly took steps in his direction.

He knew exactly when the dog saw him, because it let out a heavy, deafening bark. Once, twice, and then a third one so crisp that Silence could trace the word "fear" on the goose flesh that formed on his arms.

The dog was bigger than she had originally appeared. She had to have weighed more than Kenneth himself. Her paws, with claws that were fully stretched clutching the dirt, were as big as Kenneth's fists.

Kenneth put out his hands submissively and said, "Easy now. Go on back to Miss Hughes."

The barking came, heavy and crisp again, in a three-bark succession. By now Miss Hughes was coming up the hill, calling out to her dog.

"What is it, Honeymae? What have you found that daunts you?" She then saw him.

The dog took a decided step between Miss Hughes and Silence, and repeatedly barked three warning barks, the nature of which seemed to shake the new spring leaves from the oak.

Evelyn's face hardened, then she pointedly folded her arms. She said heatedly, "Silence."

And the dog immediately stopped barking.

How is it this woman brings me to chuckle at the drop of a hat?

"I see my name actually has use!"

She ignored his attempts at humor. "What are you doing here?"

He hadn't really planned out how he would explain his presence. "I, ah, was out riding. I hoped you made it home safely. I . . . ah, well, I suppose I came to see if you need any help."

Miss Hughes took the growling beast by the collar and energetically walked down the hill. Kenneth took the opportunity to follow her.

The cottage was a modest structure. Perhaps it had three total rooms, one of which was likely the main entrance. It only had one chimney, right in the middle. There was a middle-aged man in the garden who wore a large brimmed farmer's hat and was looking at the approaching visitor. He put his shovel down, wiped his brow, and with a rather bowlegged gait walked towards them.

Honeymae, or at least that was what Miss Hughes had called the giant monster, was still letting out deep growls that could make any man want to high-step it out of there.

But too many questions were running through his head to truly mind the beast. Who was this man who looked like a hired hand? Was this her husband? He looked at least twenty years older than Miss Hughes.

Kenneth Silence reached out his hand, and with all the charm that Spencer Kingston had taught him he offered an introduction.

"Miss Hughes, can you introduce me to your friend here? And while you are at it, can you ask your bitch to stand down? She is ready to pounce on me."

"Certainly," Miss Hughes said with a false smile and squinted eyes, which spoke more of the kind of lady he had originally deemed her to be. "Eddie Malloy, this is Mr. Silence." She released the irritating smile momentarily and snickered before she continued. "I have just thought of something from Shakespeare's *The Merchant of Venice* that fits him perfectly. You could say that 'when at his best, he is a little worse than a man, and when he is at his worst, he is little better than a beast.'"

Her drama and passion as she said it was diverting.

He cleared his throat in order to hide the chuckle, then shook Eddie's dirty hand and said, "Kenneth Silence, but just call me Silence."

He turned back to Miss Hughes. Kenneth was surprised that she would so perfectly quote *The Merchant of Venice*, so he chose one from *Henry IV*. "'Hide not thy poison with such sugar'd words.'"

Evelyn looked ponderous and said to Eddie, "As you can see, 'he is deformed, crooked, old and sere, ill-faced, worse bodied, shapeless everywhere; vicious, ungentle, foolish, blunt, unkind; stigmatical in making,' but worse of all, he is 'worse in mind.'"

That was clearly from *The Comedy of Errors.*

Kenneth vehemently scoffed but Miss Hughes ignored him, turned around, and headed to the linen line.

As Kenneth followed, Honeymae barred his path with a menacing growl that came from deep within her. "Would you be so kind to have your dog heel? I just want to converse, and I am having a hard time being polite when she is licking her chops like that. She seems to be 'a fusty nut with no kernel.'"

He waited. At first it seemed like she didn't get the last reference, but then she muttered, "*Troilus and Cressida.*"

Miss Hughes snapped her finger, and the dog obediently sat down as well and ceased the growling.

He picked up where they left off. "Very good! I did not know how well you knew Shakespeare's other works."

"'Thus sodden-witted Lord! Thou hast no more brain than I have in mine elbows.'"

"So you *do* know *Troilus and Cressida.* We might have something in common. Then again, I have yet to make out your character. 'Ye have angels' faces, but heaven knows your heart.' *Henry IV.* "

"I know where it is from. 'Your wit make wise things foolish,'"

"'Better a witty fool than a foolish wit.'"

Eddie widely smiled at the game that was taking place in front of him. He apparently decided to join in the fun and added in a heavy, Irish brogue, "I know where that one's from. Me ma always read *Twelfth Night* to me at Christmas time."

Kenneth couldn't help but enjoy this banter. She was sharp-witted, knew her Shakespeare, and if that slight gleam in her eye said anything, she was enjoying herself a little, too.

Kenneth threw one of his favorites at her. He spoke to Eddie, motioning at Miss Hughes from head to toe. "I fear you may not know it, but 'The devil hath the power to assume a pleasing shape.'" He turned to Evelyn and in a condescending tone he said, "That was from *Hamlet.*"

She huffed a bit and started taking down the bed linens that were dry, thanks to the gentle wind that morning. She attempted to fold a few of them.

Kenneth took one end of a bed sheet and started folding it with her. She looked up at him silently, a scowl on her face, but her eyes told a different story: she was grateful.

He pressed her a bit. He wasn't about to end this sassy little tête-à-tête quite yet. "What? No more abuses or affronts?"

"I was thinking of telling you something from *The Merry Wives of Windsor*. 'Go to Hell for an eternal moment or so.'"

He chuckled a bit, but then finished folding the sheet and handed it to her.

"You know, 'Thou are a wickedness'." He turned to Eddie, who had been strangely silent. "Did you catch that one?"

"Aye, heard it every Christmas. Sometimes me ma would say it when I was lazy, too."

Miss Hughes started to laugh, stifled it immediately, and reached for the next piece of linen. In a nonchalant way, she first quoted *Henry III* then immediately *As You Like It*. "'You are strangely troublesome.' Why are you here, Silence? 'I do desire we may be better strangers.'"

With this one, they both laughed a bit. Even Eddie seemed to relax a little.

"What a sweet thing to say, Miss Hughes. Here I thought we were sending three-hundred- year-old jabs at each other."

"'If I prove honey-mouthed, let my tongue blister.'"

He wasn't sure, but he thought that one was from *The Winter's Tale*. He wasn't about to ask her to clarify and lose this battle of wits.

He folded a few more well-worn dishtowels, wondering once again what brought her to the point of doing her own laundry. He hadn't failed to notice that her nails were short and her fingers looked callused. But her hair was beautifully arranged. Even when she had a bonnet on, her curls looked like they had recently been set. And now, with her bonnet off, she had ornate braids traveling from the base of her neck and crowning her head to the other side.

He couldn't imagine being able to do that kind of style without help. So who was helping her?

He looked around at the cottage. The window was open on the side of the cottage that was closest to him, but there was no other indication that anyone was here with her.

His desire and, if he was being honest, his need, to know what happened to her grew by the second.

When the laundry was done, he took the basket and started walking toward the door of the cottage.

"I will take that, sir," Miss Hughes said with a bit of anxiety.

"I do not mind. Why do you not open the door and I will place this basket wherever you desire." He definitely wanted to see inside the cottage.

She looked at the cottage frantically. Then she looked to Eddie, who seemed to understand something that was unspoken.

Eddie took the basket and said, "I know just where it goes, sir." And with that, he went towards the cottage.

Kenneth could have sworn the door was opened before Eddie got to it. So was there someone in the cottage? Someone Miss Hughes did not want him to see?

"As you can see my chores outside are competed for the day, and I must finish those on the inside. Thank you for coming. Thank you for your assistance with the linen. It was pleasant talking with you but, 'more of your conversation would infect my brain.' So, good day." She turned to leave, turned back, and was about to say something, but Kenneth said it for her.

"From *Coriolanus*."

She smiled one of the most genuine smiles he had ever seen from a lady. It started small and then fully reached her eyes, bringing a natural flush to her cheeks.

It made his breath catch in his throat slightly.

She curtsied in such a feminine way that there was no denying she was still a lady.

She was a well-bred lady, whose circumstances had drastically changed.

It rankled that he had no idea why.

BUYING THE DUKE'S SILENCE

CHAPTER 4

Evelyn closed the door to the cottage behind her and leaned against it. She could not deny that it was thrilling to spar with Mr. Silence like that. His eyes played a game that was far more enticing than any she had ever played before. She felt strangely feminine for those few moments.

Sure, she had been folding linen, a nearly daily chore, but he brought spirit to the task. For over five months she had pondered on what it felt like to be a woman, a real lady, one who did not cook and clean, or walk miles to get the vegetables she needed.

For months she had daydreamed about how Lord Tisdale had looked at her with longing, as if he was undressing her. All this time she thought that it was exciting to think a man wanted her that way.

But today brought a whole new excitement. Sparing with Silence was nothing short of thrilling, and never once did she feel undesirable, regardless of the fact that he did not have that sultry look in his eyes.

But his bright hazel eyes were absorbed, truly interested, in what she was going to say next. Not do, but say. He seemed genuinely intrigued by their conversation. There was an element of intelligence and wit that she had never felt from any other gentleman.

But there was so much that Silence did not know about her and her sister. If he did, he would have nothing to do with her. She remembered his dark hair, its natural feathers fluttering in the wind as they folded the laundry. And what kind of man starts folding linen without being asked? She felt the frustration grow and let out a sigh. She regretted succumbing to her emotions immediately as she caught her sister's eye from across the room.

"Who was that?" Ester asked.

"No one in particular. His name is Mr. Silence. But trust me, he does not live up to his name. I assure you, he is an interfering, prideful man."

She thought of his broad shoulders and tall form. She thought about his handsome hands and the way he seemed to move with grace. "Prideful *and* handsome." Evelyn's hand flew to her mouth and she gasped. *Did she really just say that?*

Eddie chuckled and said, "Where the tongue slips, it speaks the truth."

"I did not mean that! I mean he is, but you see, I cannot allow those thoughts. Like I said, he is interfering and proud. And do not forget selfish!"

Eddie's tones were exaggeratingly somber, "Aye, a proud man that assists you with yer chores and brings that smile to yer face should not be so interferin'. He said you had a pleasin' figure. He was most definitely thinking of himself. Proud, for sure."

Evelyn couldn't help but roll her eyes at his sarcasm. "Well, he did make me smile, but that means little. You, sir, have made me smile, too, and that does not mean I wish you to leave your wife and children. I grant you, he is . . . interesting."

Ester said cautiously, "Interesting? I have never known another person who loves Shakespeare as much as you, or who could keep up with your wit. Why do you not invite him over for tea?"

"Ester! You know why! He cannot . . ."

"I am not saying I have to be here for it. I could take an extended walk, or hide in the forest, or you were telling me about that tunneled—"

Evelyn sent her a sharp look.

Her sister altered the direction of the conversation immediately. "You have sacrificed so much for me. I heard you sigh when you came in. I know you would like to further the acquaintance. Trust me, he does in return. If what I heard and saw from this window was any indication, he is more than interesting. He is *interested*. And I see the difference in you. You are blushing with my words because you also know they are true."

She firmed her voice as she said, "I cannot invite him for tea. I think he is here for the duke's house party and it is ending this weekend and he will return to London. We are done talking about this. I will, however, concede that speaking with Silence was a diversion."

They both paused momentarily at the irony of the last statement. Then she proceeded to tend the household's chores, and couldn't help but dwell on the fact that she did them alone.

*****

Silence knocked on Gavin's study door. Normally he would not wait before he entered, however, the duke and duchess were known to sequester themselves and disappear for long hours. He learned after the first accidental intrusion that, with newlyweds, it may be appropriate to give them additional privacy.

He looked at his pocket watch; it was just after noon. He knocked again, this time louder, and heard muffled voices inside.

After a moment or two, the door cracked open a bit and Gavin peered at him.

"Yes, Silence?"

"Do you have a minute?"

"Is it important?"

"It is."

"What is it about?"

"Miss Hughes."

There was a flash of surprise on Gavin's face, but then he said, "Ah." Gavin looked behind him and then opened the door all the way. "Yes, come in."

Grace was sitting on the chaise, as proper as she always looked, her red hair pinned up into a neat bun. Perhaps his suspicions were unfounded. Maybe they really were just having tea.

"Good day, Your Grace," he said to Grace.

Grace smiled sweetly and asked, "Can I pour you some tea? It should still be warm."

"Yes, thank you." As she stood, he noticed that she only had one slipper on and there was a button undone on the back of her dress. It was hard not to smile.

She handed him his tea and he took a moment to drink it. It was only slightly warmer than lukewarm, but it was still refreshing.

Gavin settled into his chair behind the desk and asked, "What about Miss Hughes? I did not know you were acquainted with her."

"Yes, I met her months ago. Five, to be exact."

Gavin's face steeled a bit. "I see. And how did you meet her?"

"It was at the Halliburtons' dinner party. Very interesting party."

"Yes, I hear their parties always are. I am sorry I missed it."

It seemed that Gavin was being vague, because it seemed he knew exactly which party he was referring to. It wasn't that the duke was lying, just being rather evasive. He was clearly uncomfortable with the conversation, as evidenced by the stiffness in his back as well as how he stole a glance at his wife before answering Kenneth.

Kenneth kept his senses piqued and asked directly, "Have you seen her recently?"

Gavin looked at Grace once again, looked down at the papers on his desk, moved the ink well, and without looking at Kenneth said, "I have not seen her for some time."

His brows darkened; it wasn't a lie. But it wasn't the truth, either.

"And what about you, Grace?" he probed.

"Me? Oh, I cannot say when the last time I saw her was."

Again, it was the truth, yet evasive. She probably truly *couldn't* "say" when she saw her last, but it was deceiving nonetheless.

Kenneth thought he would poke a bit harder. "Grace, has Gavin here told you about me? About what gifts I possess?"

70

She looked down at her hands and nodded.

Gavin interrupted him before he asked his next question. "Silence, what are you about? Do not beat around the bush or fish for more than has been given. Grace is aware you can detect truth versus lies."

He turned back to Gavin. He delivered his question directly this time. "How do you know Miss Hughes?"

Gavin explained stiffly, "Miss Hughes is my mother's goddaughter. I have known her all her life. I would say she is like a sister to me. I have not seen her for many weeks."

Truth. Darn. All of it.

He felt the frustration from not knowing turn into a low, simmering anger. "But you saw her a few weeks ago? And did you know she is living in a small cottage on Fleetwood Place land? Alone, no less, unless that Irishman is supposed to be with her, but I doubt that. Who is he anyway?"

His friend took a deep breath. "Silence, Silence."

A small grin sprung up on all their faces at Gavin's play on his name. "In truth, I cannot answer any of your questions but one: yes, I know she is there."

"And the Irishman?"

Gavin gave him a stern look. "I told you what I am free to tell. Please let it go."

Kenneth looked at Gavin a moment longer, and changed the subject. "I do not think I will be staying much longer."

"What about Jane Hadlock?" Grace asked hopefully.

"I find I have some business that I need to attend to."

The voice of warning came again from Gavin. "Do not do it. I know you. I see it in your eyes. You want to research Miss Hughes. I warn you, take off your investigator hat. It is important that no one knows she is here. You probably assessed that much."

"Yes, and you also know that I have to do it. The truth is out there. She left society five months ago. Granted, I did not care enough to give it much notice, but she is doing hard labor, like laundry, and buying her own market vegetables! Her formerly soft hands now have calluses on them! How can you say you know about this and not assist? Can you not even spare a maid? She is all alone there!"

Gavin leaned on his hands, then stood. The look in his friend's eyes was the look of a titled duke.

Silence wasn't one to back down, and gave him a look that was just as stern.

It was a battle of both pride and wills that only exceedingly great friends could endure for the length that they did without resulting in a meeting at dawn with pistols.

Silence had practically challenged Gavin, implying he would treat his mother's goddaughter with such little consideration. And Gavin was asking him to back down. But there was no greater champion of honor and truth than Silence.

It was the ultimate battle of wills because both passionately felt they were right. Silence knew that a true lady in need should be taken care of, no matter the reason. Gavin probably felt that Silence was not going to heed the counsel to not investigate.

It was sticky, and volatile, but Silence put his teacup down on the desk without breaking eye contact.

Kenneth Silence declared, "I have to. You know I do."

"Do not do it."

"Then tell me."

His friend sighed. "I cannot."

"Then I have urgent business in London. I am sorry to leave your party early. I was going to stay a bit longer, but I will leave tomorrow morning."

Gavin looked down and then glanced at his wife. She nodded reassuringly. Gavin gave a subtle shake of his head, exhaled again heavily, then turned to Kenneth.

"Silence, do me a favor: do not disclose her location. I know you have your own agency, and it is a stubborn one at that. But you know me well enough to know that I would never let any harm come to her. I am assisting as much as I am allowed. Eddie Malloy is a hired hand I have procured to protect—" he paused as if he was about to say something he wasn't supposed to, or at the very least had already done so. Then Gavin finished, saying, "—her."

"You have my word. Her location will not be revealed."

*****

The next morning he thought he would take the scenic route, and made his way in the wee hours of the morning towards the cottage. He wasn't expecting to see her; after all, it was just past dawn, but the pale blue gown looked ghostly as it fluttered in the wind.

Miss Hughes was gently swinging under a giant oak. Her hair was completely down, swishing forward and backwards with the movement of the swing. It was enchanting to see her red curls' spirit unleashed and freely whipping one way and then another. Her gown would cling to her thin but shapely legs as she moved forward, and billowed like a pillow as she swung backwards. He slowed Nimbus and dismounted, causing a bit of noise, which he immediately regretted since it startled her, bringing her attention to himself.

He took off his hat and bowed. "Good morning, Miss Hughes. Do not stop swinging. I did not mean to disturb you."

She, of course, as stubborn as she was, immediately stopped. However, she did not dismount from the swing. Her hands clung to the rope on both sides of her face, leaving her hair to cascade down her front and back. With no words she just looked at him, a question in her eyes.

His voice came out a bit hoarse. "I am headed back to London."

"I see. This is a bit off the road to London. I would say you like to take the path less traveled."

I believe the saying is a road *less traveled.*

The suspicious rise of her eyebrow reminded him of why he was there. He hoped that his cheeks were not as scarlet as he felt they were.

He cleared his throat and walked behind her, hoping to buy himself a moment outside of her vision to let the heat in his cheeks dissipate. But seeing her red curls cascade down her back, nearly to her waist, was not helpful by half. He did manage to restrain himself from reaching out and touching the curls that had somehow managed to catch the first rays of sun, making them glow as if she was from the hereafter.

He managed to walk to the trunk of the tree, put his hat in the crook of a branch, and leaned against the bulk of the tree.

As casually as he could, he put one foot up against the tree and folded his arms. He certainly didn't feel relaxed, but he thought he should at least portray it with his posture.

He realized he still had not answered her. "No, this is not a natural stop on the way to London. But you have puzzled me greatly, Miss Hughes. I cannot help but be curious. I spoke with the duke, and he could only offer me the smallest assurance that he was taking care of you. You are doing work that a servant would do. I cannot help but wonder why."

She smiled slightly at him, and then returned her gaze ahead of her. "I have my reasons. And I should tell you, it is not as bad as a servant's life. I am learning a great deal. I am mastering things that I would never have been allowed to learn."

"Pray tell, what do you speak of? To cook and clean?"

"Well, yes, but that is not what I was referring to."

"Laundry then?" he said with a grin. "I see the appeal . . . the smell of the lye soap, the scalding-hot water, but I have to say—"

She giggled slightly. "Trust me, I could do without ever knowing how to do laundry, and I would still find happiness."

"Then you are happy?"

She silently started swinging again. With her legs pumping, she leaned back and forth to get the motion going.

When he thought she would not answer him, she finally slowed her legs and let the motion take her back and forth.

He noticed the smallest of sighs before she answered, "I am content. And in return, I find others are happy. And that is good enough for me."

He dissected this bit of information before asking his next question. "So you are sacrificing your happiness for the sake of others? All this," he indicated, motioning to the vastness of the untamed part of the duke's land. "For whom?"

Her eyes flickered to him with surprised concern. It was clear she said more than she'd intended, or at the very least she was surprised that he deducted as much of the truth as he did.

He definitely did not want to make her uncomfortable, so he reluctantly stood and picked up his hat from the crook of the tree.

Glancing at her lovely form as it swayed was one delight he knew he must not partake of. At least not anymore than he already had.

He tipped his hat and said, "Good day, Miss Hughes. I pray you will find happiness, for yourself as well as for whomever you love so unconditionally."

With that, he bowed and mounted Nimbus. There was a remarkable ache in his chest as he turned the horse away.

Maybe she wasn't so selfish or entitled.

Maybe she was not a proud elitist whose only goal was to trap the highest titled man into marriage.

His confusion rose to alarming levels, and he did not like being so muddled. He had no answers for what brought Miss Evelyn Hughes' circumstances so low, but he knew one thing.

As the ache grew with the distance between them, he knew he had an irrational desire to make her situation better.

BUYING THE DUKE'S SILENCE

CHAPTER 5

Evelyn watched him mount and gallop away again. The horse crested the hill and disappeared as it went down the slope.

The wind picked up and sent powerful chills through her. At least she thought it was the wind.

She had stopped pumping her legs for some time and so there was only the slightest movement of the swing, but even that seemed to make her stomach uneasy.

Or maybe she felt like she was going to cast up her accounts because she hadn't eaten yet that morning. She stood up, intending to head to the cottage, but found she was mindlessly following after Silence instead.

At the top of the hill she was shocked to see him at the bottom, where he had dismounted and was pacing agitatedly. He had not ridden far.

She watched him curiously, because whatever he was wrestling with was significant. Every once in a while he would kick a rock intensely and send it rolling away. He would turn to Nimbus and say something with energy, but she was too far from him to hear more than muted murmurs. She knew that he felt passion about what he said, but couldn't fathom the topic.

Finally, after more than ten minutes, he put one hand on the saddle horn, paused before mounting, then bowed his head as if he was defeated.

Her heart ached for him for some reason. She hated to see anyone in such turmoil, but she did not know how to help him.

She heard Honeymae's large paws prancing behind her. Her dog had sniffed out her location, and was probably hungry. The great beast placed her snout into her hand and she rubbed its head.

Suddenly Honeymae growled and let out one of her deep barks. Panic seized her, as she knew that Silence would look at the source of the bark. Her protector continued with the other two barks that she knew would follow.

She was frozen as Silence slowly looked up the hill toward her. He altered the defeated stance he had taken, stood upright, and brushed his hands through his hair one more time, then replaced his hat.

They stared at each other for a few seconds, neither one acknowledging why he had not continued on to the road toward London, nor why she had followed after him to watch him leave.

There were no answers, and that left all the questions hanging in the misty air.

At nearly the same moment they both turned, leaving to go the path they had intended before this stolen moment in the foggy morning.

Her nausea was gone. And it was replaced with a strangely comforting curiosity about Kenneth Silence.

But she doubted that her questions would burn off as fast as the fog would.

*****

It had been two weeks since he returned to London, and he had completed two investigations, been compensated quite nicely for one, and let the other slide since it was concluded so quickly. But the first income was hefty and more than satisfactory, which allowed him to buy the painting by the late William Burgess he had been admiring, as well as a new, lighter fabric great coat that would be more comfortable in the summer heat.

Silence kept himself busy with the correspondence he was usually behind on by several weeks.

He did not much like personal letter writing, and in fact only did it when forced. His job forced him to write far too many letters of inquiry as it was, so he never had the urge to spend more time with quill in hand.

No one would dare accuse Kenneth of procrastinating. But as he wrote the fourth personal letter that morning, not to mention the five the day before, it was clear to him that he was avoiding something.

He put the quill down and dusted the fresh script.

He knew darn well what he was avoiding.

He didn't want to think about Miss Evelyn Hughes.

But it was no use. She was obstinate and invasive, no matter his efforts of distraction. In the rare moments he allowed himself to think on the issue, he just got more confused.

He trusted Gavin and Grace. They admitted they knew she was on their land. Eddie Molloy was there to protect her. But why did she need to be protected, or why did she need more protection than her own father's home could provide? And how much protection could one farm hand offer a single lady?

That brought up other concerns. Did the door actually open when Eddie brought in the laundry, and if so, who else was living with her? Was she forced to marry? Had she been shunned from society?

He had been too afraid to start the inquiry of her known associates. He wasn't entirely sure why. What if he found out things that could unintentionally harm her? Or confirm those nagging suspicions that he desperately did not want to know were true.

Could she be with . . . no, certainly not; she was as thin as she was five months ago.

He continued to massage what pieces he knew, and flesh out what he did not.

Gavin specifically asked that he not give away her location. So she was in hiding?

He recalculated the direction his thoughts were heading.

If she was living with someone, who could it be? Who was worth sacrificing her happiness for? He deliberated about how she had given her answer some thought before saying that she was not happy, but rather "content", as long as it made others happy.

This loving, selfless act did not seem to match what he had originally assessed in her character.

So who was the real Evelyn Hughes?

And why did she seem so cautious?

She was not the only one who appeared to have knowledge of something he did not know, which was quite rare. Unnervingly so.

He folded the letter and sealed it, allowing a bit too much wax to melt in his distraction.

He leaned back and rubbed his eyes. He was tired of not making sense of this mystery. But where should he start? And how would he go about making the inquiries without raising questions in others? It was a delicate issue, and he knew it.

If he just took another week or two to ponder it, maybe he would know the answers.

That was what he did.

*****

Evelyn memorized the beautiful pattern of the bird's flight; its pattern of flying up, then gracefully taking the wind down, tilting one way, then the other. And just before the fowl would have landed it fluttered with exertion in another great ascent towards the clouds, only to repeat it again.

Over and over again the thoughts came and went, in and out. How much work did the bird endure as it sought the highest height, only to appear to suddenly want nothing more than to fall unaided by anything but its own wings?

What if her wings failed her?

She worked on her thoughts with similar intensity. At the intense moment that she could work no harder to fight them, she let herself enjoy the moment where she felt the exhilarating free fall. Silence was strangely addicting; there was always the surprise, rush of curiosity, challenge of intellect, and then . . . the confusion.

And again the cycle continued, just like the bird. She fought with all her might to escape the imaginary foe. For her, instead of flapping her wings like the bird, she made sure to remember all of the pompous, interfering, self-centered inferences.

And to complete the pattern, the free fall in recalling the diverting smirk she had put on his face during the battle of Shakespearean affronts.

But her thoughts always came full circle with the confusion. Why did he travel over three miles out of his way to say his farewells?

The duke's estate wasn't so far, at least not as the bird flies. She laughed at this thought, considering the metaphor she had just used to help sort out her thoughts and feelings.

It was probably less than a mile, but there was no easy path for cart or horse to traverse the boulders or the cavern between them. So for him to have intended to see her he had to take the only possible path, around the boulders at the opening of the cavern—which she knew was the shortest path—but even with a horse, the three miles could take an hour in the pre-dawn darkness.

So did he just want to give his farewells? Or did he revel in witnessing her trials? Yet it was dawn, and even servants do not do chores . . . She let her mind begin the exertion to fight against gravity, just like the bird.

And so the cyclic assent resumed, not realizing the intent was to get to that moment where she felt the free fall.

She heard the clomp of work boots, only minimally muted due to the amount of mud on them.

"You'll never plow a field by turnin' it over in yer mind," Eddie said, while at the same time shoving yesterday's crusted-over bread into his mouth.

"Is that another of your mum's sayings?"

"Nah, me pa's. He meant it, too. Jus' like I do." He ticked his head to the right towards the open door, where there was a decent view of a plow horse with his head low, as if he knew what would be asked of him today.

It was the same as would be asked of her.

"Sorry, Miss Hughes. I do wish I wasn't . . . I mean, I ain't really . . . it don't matter. Yer pa wouldn't 'ave let me anyhow." Eddie was kicking the mud off his right boot with the left.

Her heart dropped for her friend, for that is what he had become. For almost six months Eddie had been protector, servant, the forager of mushrooms, the roof thatcher, the man of Irish idioms, and he had most definitely become her friend. Her enormously tall friend. She rarely saw him inside the cottage, but with him having to stoop slightly she realized just how tall he was.

Evelyn offered a rescuing solution to his discomfort. "I feel I could use some fresh air today. Eddie, would you mind sweeping in here for the morning? It could use a fresh mopping and a bit of the waxing cream. Someone seemed to drag a great deal of mud in on their work boots."

A small, guilty smile rose on the Irishman's lips and he said, "I suppose I should do that before I plow?"

"Most definitely. And since it does not look like it would be too much bother, might you catch the corners of the ceiling with a cloth? The soot has built up again."

He looked up at the one corner he could see with his head bent as it was, and added, "Aye, it 'as."

She started towards the door, but he stopped her. He looked down at his worn, tattered, wide-brimmed farmer's hat and he placed it on her head. "The sun is high. Yer a fair-skinned lady, and I think this'll protect you better than the silly frillies you put together with yer sister."

She placed her hand on his arm and delivered a comforting squeeze. "You protect me best. Allow me to show my appreciation. I might have a mind to go riding, too, if that old draft horse can handle the likes of me."

She walked past him with her head high.

She had never plowed a field before.

And more than likely, Eddie had never attempted plowing again ever to since he saw his father fall under the horse. He had been barely twelve.

But Eddie knew she could do it, so she knew she could do it. She knew what a horse needed, and she had it in her to give.

She tried not to wrinkle her nose at the smell the hat brought with it, and the work it represented, because it was robust and distinctively musky. No doubt she would have a similar aroma, and perhaps would be just as foul at the end of the task she was about to perform.

As she exited the cottage, she heard Eddie call out, "Miss? Might you leave the door open? Jus' in case?"

There would be no "just in case", she thought. But she did so anyway.

As she guided the horse, she examined the animal. The girth of the shoulders and belly was impressive; he was almost the same diameter from the withers through the meeting of the hindquarters. This horse was solid; old, but solid.

She was quite familiar with saddling a riding mare, but the plow harnesses that were already attached were unfamiliar. It appeared the main part focused on connecting a well-padded strap on the chest to the belly band, which didn't look too much different than the ones on her saddle.

Someone, most likely Eddie, had made sure it was clear on what to do. Both bands were connected in two major areas on each side of the horse. The upper connection appeared to simply be a very long pair of reins. The lower one, however, was a long, thick wooden pole, and attached to a strappy harness near its loins and rear flank.

The plow itself was already on the north end of the small field, ready to do the first length. She hardly had to guide the horse at all; it seemed to sense what to do. She hooked up the hitch, hoping she remembered all the steps Eddie had mentioned last night.

She walked behind the plow, took a firm hold of the plow's handles, and waited.

She called out to the horse, "Hiyah!" But nothing happened other than a stomp of the hooves and a slight tug on the lower lines from the movement. She almost called again, before she realized that she did not have the reins.

The horse knew it, too.

She unrolled the reins, tossing the one on the other side as she walked past. It was impossible to see over the top of the horse's high end, so when she got to the plow she had to lay one line down, then go around and collect the other.

With little more than a slight flicker the horse moved forward, head low. Once he started, he found a pace. It was a slow enough pace for her to manage her footing on the freshly turned dirt. The plow's handles were just a bit high for her, and she found she had to use some of her weight to keep the nose of the plow where it needed to be. The horse could have been using an architect's square as a guide for how intensely, and accurately, it was moving in a straight line. It was simply a matter for her to keep the nose of the share where it needed to be.

In no time at all, she had plowed her first cornrow. The next question was, how was she supposed to turn the horse around?

She flicked the reins on the right then pulled only the right, hoping it would turn, but the horse would have none of it. It raised his head proudly and danced slightly, a step forward, then backwards, making her lose balance on the plow.

She tried with all her might but the plow tipped over, lifting out of the wet dirt.

She started to lift it upright, when the horse started walking again, turning south. She tried to guide the horse with the reins, telling it to stop, when she realized that in getting the plow turned over, the horse had just shown her how to turn without exerting nearly as much effort.

The horse had found his place, but slightly to the outside of the run she had just plowed. She walked toward the front and tried to reposition it.

The stubborn horse just kept moving to the position it previously had taken. It seemed the horse simply did not want to walk with one side of hooves in the overturned dirt and the other on the winter-pressed ground.

She had spent all of twenty minutes adjusting the horse and plow, pushing and pulling. Finally, she just let it do what it wanted.

It was so foreign to how she was taught to ride by her father.

To him, it was important that the horse knew you were in charge. That *you* held the reins. That it was *you* who said to stop. That *you* were dominant. He taught her that the way you appeared on a horse amongst society said everything about what your value should be to the world.

For the first time in many months she was grateful no one could see her follow the horse's lead, for she had significantly sunk in value in the last few months.

She halted the self-pity immediately, and reached deep inside for the good that could be found of having no control over this animal.

We may not have perfectly straight rows, but perhaps this horse shall instinctually make the perfect corn maze, and getting lost in it shall be far more fun than this.

After taking a moment to catch her breath from laughing, not to mention fighting with the horse on his position, she took the lines up behind the plow, threw them over her shoulders, and resigned to have an unevenly plowed garden.

With the mere lift of the reins, the horse moved forward. She guided the share's nose deep into the ground as the old horse pulled with his head low. Again, it seemed all she had to do was keep the share deep in the ground, shifting her weight from one handle to the other to ensure it did so.

Halfway through the run she had to lean quite significantly to the left to stay straight, and in doing so her odiferous, gifted hat blew off.

She looked back behind her for the hat, and realized that the horse had known all along where he was to plow. The turning of the dirt, with the horse's feet fully on the winter-pressed, unplowed dirt, had perfectly tilled the unplowed dirt. The angle of the share, with its thick V-shaped blade, began its turbulence of the dirt several inches from the edge of the previous row. However, as the dirt was pulled and rolled over the metal lips that extended laterally on both sides of the share's blade, there was no earth that hadn't been turned over in the run so far.

This time she laughed, lifting her face to the sun. She knew she would regret it, but she would rather get burned than wear that oversized, offensive stink on her red hair.

Through the day, she continued the same pattern of tipping the plow over slightly at the end, allowing it to lift from the depths of the soil, then rotating the horse around, ensuring the blade went deep and straight for the next run.

It was hard, and it was work.

It wasn't long until she understood why a man wore wide brimmed hats. And as she wiped the perspiration from her forehead she understood other benefits of the hat as well and, of course, a full explanation of the stench.

She most definitely could not wait until Sunday for her weekly bath. She would give up next week's water, if she could clean the grime off before nightfall.

The field was over halfway plowed, but she felt she had met her match. Not just because she was at her physical limit of what she could handle, but the clouds promised a shorter workday. How grateful she was at that moment for rain. The wind that accompanied the clouds was a much-needed friend, and helped her push through another two rows before the rain started. She finally tipped the plow to the side, tossed the right lead towards the front, and walked the left lead around.

The horse was breathing as heavily as she was, its nostrils flaring with each breath, and a thick frothy line of secretions had formed around its muzzle and lips. It was attempting to lap at the scattered rain.

Her soul was flooded with intense guilt. She knew all too well how taxed she was, with bleeding blisters on her palms and aching shoulders, but she had never once considered the horse was doing almost all of the work.

She made quick work of disconnecting the plow from the animal, and brought it to the water trough. He began lapping at the pool at once. She did not wait half a second more to collapse on the nearest place to sit; the thick log that Eddie used to chop wood. She rubbed one shoulder with her hand, rotating the angry joint as she did so. She had asked more from herself in one day than she had ever done in a month.

Her skin was raw in so many ways.

Her feet had never known such heat and hatred for overuse.

Her nose was resisting true, clear breath, for what she only assumed was from dirt-encrusted narrowing.

Her arms alone, if not asked to do another thing for weeks, would still offer no forgiveness.

The small of her back seemed to make more noise than Honeymae trying to protect her. Each joint of that small curve screaming, as if it could take her giant dog on by its barking ache alone.

After her bath, there would be nothing left in her. She knew this assuredly, and closed her eyes briefly. If only she could rest a moment longer before the rain set in fully. The cooler air was appreciated, but the fat drops stung her sunburned arms and face.

Her tired lids lifted for a moment and only stared at the plow blade, which was terribly encrusted with dirt and grime. The horse alone would take an hour to brush out.

She bowed her head and whispered, "I should have thought of the animal earlier. My father would have never . . ." her voice trailed off. She simply couldn't finish.

"No, he would not," Eddie said.

That was not the first time she had the desire to humble his ever-present stubborn, self-righteous, Irish opinion.

Even as startled as she was, her head could not have shot up even if she asked it to. "He would not quit," she grumbled back at Eddie.

She vaguely saw him look to his right. "Ester, might you see if the bath water is ready?"

This lifted her head enough to see her sweet sister, smiling with a mixture of pride, sorrow, guilt, and gratitude.

Ester said, "I'm quite sure it is. Come, Evie, it is finished; you have done enough."

Eddie and Ester each came to her, one on each side. Everywhere they touched screamed in pain, and yet the tenderness seemed to be a balm to her soul. As they walked past the filthy V-shaped spade that she had spent all day walking behind, she opened her mouth to protest.

Eddie interrupted, "I been cleanin' tools me whole life, Miss. And I might not like to use it, on account of me pa, but I know when a work animal has had enough. And you, me dear, have had enough."

"But my father would have . . ."

"Yes, Miss Evelyn. But you've got to do yer own growing, no matter how tall yer father was." His brogue was thick, which is the only thing that alerted her to the fact that it was an Irish saying.

"I think I'll try to figure that one out later. It sounded wise, like I should remember it, or at the very least understand why you recited it to me."

"Thank you kindly."

Intense confusion regarding the Irish idiom was the last thing she remembered clearly. Keeping her eyes closed seemed to cool the dry, irritated orbs.

She sensed that her sister may have bathed her, only because the irritating dirt particles were no longer demanding a voice of their own with each step or movement of a joint.

She wasn't aware of the exact moment when her body surrendered to the draw of newly washed sheets.

Thank you, Ester. Thank you, Eddie.

She muttered one more thing: "Thank you, God."

CHAPTER 6

"I don't rightly know, sir."

"THAT IS NOT GOOD ENOUGH!"

The ratty-haired vagrant flinched like his life was on the line.

Good. At least he knows I mean business.

And he did mean business; he could not mean it any more. Tears or not, that boy had better find her.

"I undastand. I ain't gonna disappoint yer majesty."

He grabbed the boy's shirt in his fist, pulling him in, making sure his height did the communicating. As calmly as possible, he said, "Don't call me that. It isn't even accurate."

"No, sir. You are right, sir, me Lord, yer Grace."

It maddened him that the street rat said "sir" like "suuaah". Everything about him irritated him. He opened his pocket watch and saw he was out of time.

Turning to leave he tossed the smallest coin he had, and muttered his command: "Find her."

As he left, he threw off the old tattered cloak. If the boy was smart, he'd sell it.

*****

Kenneth's walk to White's was invigorating and, as always, enlightening. It is interesting the facts he learns through his gift.

Apparently, Miss Mary Jacobs really was cheating on her intended. And her "friend" she was walking out her side door lied about not only his name, but he was not there as her solicitor either.

The Johnsons actually loathed each other, but he didn't need his talent to understand that. Their boisterous argument was–

– passionately honest. It would not surprise him if one of them harmed the other.

Kenneth Silence thanked the Johnsons in his mind as their voices trailed off behind him. Their passionate quarrel had lightened his headache a bit.

His head basically always ached.

Why couldn't people be honest, or at least speak freely to each other?

Sometimes he wanted to scream, "Take off the masks! Let people know you!"

Other times, he just wanted to beg people to "say what you mean and mean what you say." Both offenses caused just as much ache.

He knew something that many people did not know about themselves. Most people actually *wanted* to tell the truth. They needed—it was an extremely powerful human need—to be known.

But they had been taught by society that no one wanted to hear how bad their day really was, or how they might lose their family home.

It is also why thieves and murderers returned to the scene of the crime. There was a part of them that wanted to be found out. When someone returned to the scene, in that miniature moment they did not have to pretend, or at least remember, what fiction they created to sustain for others.

Yes, people wanted to tell the truth.

But they didn't.

It scared them. They had thoughts like: *"If the Johnsons could kill each other, is it possible when my husband starts yelling that he could, too?"* Or, *"My wife tosses money out the window with a teaspoon, faster than I can bring it through the front door with a shovel. Could we lose our home, too, like them?"*

They would rather talk about what they want their life to be like.

Which means they lied, constantly. And it gave him a constant headache.

And he hated lies.

No, that wasn't entirely correct. He hated the headaches. The lies didn't bother him because, with his gift, he would always still know the truth. He just wished he didn't get the headache.

The best part about his path to White's was the tavern at the intersection one block before it, called The Pub. The Pub had cheaper ale, more robust company, and the gossip wasn't so dry. He ordered his usual spiced cider.

His mind returned to its earlier ruminations. The truth was, those who had few possessions or status already acknowledged it, and didn't pretend to be more than they are. This was mostly because that was all they knew, and that meant it was usually enough. And when they did talk about being more than they are, they were simply sharing their dreams. *Goodness, how refreshing the poor are.*

He took this favorite metal garden seat at the shop's front entrance, right on the cobblestone street that had been closed at this time of night to accommodate the busy night-time foot traffic in this district.

He loved this intersection of town.

Silence was on the corner of Fame, Greed, Honor, and Filth.

Down one street was the theatre district.

Down another was White's, and therefore the elitists who must mention they attended the establishment, who they broke bread with, and what bets had been placed, in all tomorrow's social endeavors.

And he could not ignore the building behind him, closed for the day, but still majestically situated. It was intended to be a neutral meetinghouse for solicitors and barristers, but ended up being used entirely by the House of Commons as an unspoken negotiation and "buying" market. It is where votes were bought and sold, or not.

And he could always tell who had been bought and who had not. He didn't need his gift for that. Any person could tell by the way they walked.

He heard a joke once.

"How do you know it is cold in London?"

"Because you see attorneys with their hands in their own pockets."

But truthfully, that was how one could tell. When you have money, a lot of money, you hold it until you are safely home.

Those who did not get bought had hands free to help others, like the lady getting out of the carriage, or to tip a hat to those you respect.

The rest, well, they were bound by the money that bought them.

He continued his metaphorical examination of the intersection. He need not even turn to the right, for the odor drifted up from the street urchins, this time a bit musky, and he could see from the side that some poor lad was being forced by his father to eat "humble pie". And as the wind drifted from their direction, he could tell the pie had far too much cloves.

If Kenneth could smell it from here the boy either had a terrible toothache, or his father had rubbed his nose in the spice—and that burns—which could account for the boy's tears. Luckily the usually pleasant aroma departed as fast as it came, and so did the father's loud lecture that should have been done in private.

He hoped his spiced cider would still be palatable after that overwhelming wave of cloves.

Yes, Silence was on the corner of Fame, Greed, Honor, and Filth. But he had discovered that it was where truth was found. The lies that brought everyone to this spot, and the simple alchemy of it all, eventually revealed those little white fibs like draining the dirty bathwater. Each of them exposed for their inner truth.

The irony of it was that, for each person trapped by their lies, whether it was reaching for Fame, Greed, Honor, or Filth, must make their choice as to which path to take to leave this intersecting medley of desires. Most chose to go the way they came. If they sought fame they returned to seeking it, and therefore the lies.

He glanced back toward the quarreling father and son, and noticed an acute contradiction to his long developed theory.

The father had throw off the cloak. The son turned one direction, toward Honor, but the father turned toward none other than White's. Greed.

Things just got interesting.

Of course, he straightway had to go to White's, too.

*****

"Mr. Thomas! Sir! Come quick, there's a post from Miss Ester! But ma ain't got no coin to accept it!"

Phillip Thomas felt he had only been asleep for an hour. After docking so late last night, he hadn't so much as taken his shoes off or his overcoat, which meant his coins were on him.

Hearing that he had words from Ester was like getting thrown into the sea from your bunk. Your head cleared with a natural flood of energy. And having been at sea for three weeks, with no word, was trying. His last letter was full of Ester's sorrow and guilt for having to watch her sister plow a field. He did have to admit that Evelyn had changed. Who would have thought that she could become so selfless, so compassionate? Ester had tried to tell him it was true, that she had always been that kind of person, but he only saw what Evelyn shared in public circles. That "Miss Hughes" was not entirely admirable.

He followed after, easily keeping up with the lad's youthful energy. He had a bit of his own.

How was she faring in the summer heat?

He paid for the post but immediately sensed it was not from Esther, but rather her sister, Evelyn. At first he was disappointed, but then dread sank in.

Oh no! Please no.

He tore it open, trying to put a cap on his panic.

Dear Phillip,

 Forgive me for taking the liberty of writing, everything is well. But I have found that certain burdens are not enticing to carry alone. In fact, I would much rather discharge it to someone else. But as you know, we only have Eddie. He has spent hours in the garden, slaving away in the morning to avoid the afternoon.

Little sprouts are popping up everywhere, and I mean everywhere. Some will be ready to harvest in less than two months, but we are taking great care to nurture them. Most tolerate the whole day without appearance of distress. But the nights find them restless and souls droopy. But there is always promise of sun.

Speaking of which, may I offer my congratulations regarding your new post! Assistant to the captain! You must tell us more than, "Three-to four-week stretches, with a two-week break before we sail." Since my sister has been filtering through the fishing basket that she stores all of your earlier letters in as if she might find one she hasn't read one hundred times already, I'm going to assume you have been at sea. I have taken the liberty of telling her as much.

Now that you know you are missed, and we are all waiting on a healthy, robust harvest, I must share with you my purpose in writing.

As you know, Honeymae is a giant lazy dog; that is, if I am in eyesight. The moment she hears me even hint of moving to another part of the house or move outside, she follows me like a shadow, a big shadow, since she weighs almost three or five stone more than me. Perhaps I am unreasonable, but there have been at least four times where she is nowhere in sight! She always returns, but once it was at night. She wasn't even in the house, nor was she at the front door, standing watch. She always comes back unharmed. I suppose she is getting adventurous, and the duke's land is by far more thrilling to explore than London streets and its potted gardens. I just thought I would let you know.

Sincerely,
Miss Evelyn Hughes

*****

She knew she was dreaming. At least she thought so. She was told once that if you can direct the dream with your mind, or your choices in the dream, then you really are dreaming.

Everyone around her was passing by, as if she were invisible. But she wore a gown she had never worn before, let alone could imagine. Its needlework must have taken three years alone. No doubt it was as unique as . . .

As what? She filtered through her mind, looking for just the right metaphor. What in her life was unique? Her situation? Probably not so uncommon. Her hair? True, her strawberry-blonde hair had once been unique, but after six months of minimal care it lacked luster, and would only be noticed for her stalwart attempts to tame it without a lady's maid.

But before she could find a metaphor, the dream shifted. She was back at that pianoforte at the Halliburtons dinner party. The room seemed brighter, warmer, and yet she was more anxious than she had ever been. The room held more people than she remembered. Yet, no one seemed to notice her. It was like she was invisible. As if she could disappear and no one would ever know she was gone.

Strangely, she seemed to enjoy it. Being invisible. She was not being scrutinized by every person, whose words were foreign to the language of their body. As she moved through the crowd she could hear their thoughts; so cheap, and shallow, and judgmental. It was strangely funny. It was strangely unnerving. She felt a twinge in her chest, and it suddenly hurt to breathe. It was strangely familiar, too.

She needed out. She needed some fresh air. In her dream she searched for the exit, only to run into Silence and that horrid cigar smoke.

She startled awake. The night was heavy with humidity, and its heat was horrid. She had hoped for a reprieve from the day's heat. The dream lingered as if it, too, held weight that would only continue to crush her lungs like the humidity.

She could hear Ester breathing heavily a few feet away. It had to be hard on her, too. Her glass of water at her bedside was half-full. Evelyn always made sure her sister had a full one before retiring.

Evelyn slipped into her tattered slippers, old dancing slippers that she had cut out the back of the heel so she could have something to wear at night. As much as they cleaned, the house was not entirely secure from critters and vermin.

As she stood, her mind simultaneously cleared from the dreamlike state.

She froze. She felt an instinctual sharpened alertness, and it confused her more than scared her.

She went and opened the front door. It creaked, just as loud as ever.

She turned back around, wondering where Honeymae was. Her dog was like her shadow in the house, especially at night. At the base of her front door was a basket of market vegetables and a slab of what she presumed was meat, considering it was packaged similarly to the meat from the butcher.

She felt uneasy for a moment, Honeymae would have never left that wrapped meat unattended if she had been outside.

She clicked her tongue twice. Nothing. She moved further outside, and thought she heard Honeymae on the side of the house. But her mastiff was not on the side of the house.

She continued, but the night was so dark she had to watch the ground as she moved around to the rear of the house, where there were more trees. That area often stayed cooler than any other part of the immediate grounds around the cottage.

She glanced into the trees, but soon found that wasn't so prudent. Eddie wasn't that great about putting away his tools. She took a deep breath and pushed through the throbbing on her toes.

She kept clicking her tongue, calling for her dog while babying her right foot. When that didn't bring Honeymae, she patted her outer thigh twice.

Finally, she called for her in a whisper. "Honey! Come here, girl."

Another twig cracked, but from behind, a few yards back. And then heavy human footfalls could be heard. She dared not turn around.

Hopefully she was still dreaming.

No one should be here. Not on the cottage land. But if they were, it was too late for her.

Then, when nothing happened when she expected it, she slowly turned around to face the owner of the footfalls.

*****

White's was just as painful as it had always been.

Silence acknowledged his father's cousin, even chatted with him a bit, but then moved through the crowd and noticed a few younger gentlemen who looked foxed.

Perfect. He moved that direction.

He should feel guilty, but he didn't. Liquor loosened the tongue, and if they did not speak the truth at least their lies sounded like bedtime stories.

He was only half-listening to their recent conquests and "achievements of a lifetime" because he was still perplexed on where the father who had been yelling at the boy had gone.

He hadn't done more than turn away to chug his own spiced cider and slap a coin on the table. But when he turned around to follow the spicy man he was gone, yet his scent still lingered. He followed the scent all the way to White's, but then it had evaporated into the familiar expensive cigar smoke, port, and imported whiskey that defined White's atmosphere.

He focused again on the conversation of the gloaters and the other men lusting over the juiciest story. Suddenly he was welcomed into the group, as if he had just walked up, when in reality he had stepped into their circle of manliness about seven minutes prior.

"Silence! Are you ill?" Sir Richard asked loudly.

Furrowing his brow, he answered, "I do not think so."

"Well. I was just telling my nephew here, I know, he looks older than I do, but remember, I do have a sister who is 17 years older than me!"

Everyone around the table laughed at the ridiculous statement of fact that was said as if it was a punch line.

"And?" Silence asked.

He knew he was in a foul mood. He had never, ever, tailed someone and lost them.

"And wyyhhhaaat?" Sir Richard's last word slurring into three syllables. The confusion spread like wildfire in the whole sodden group.

His friend's head swayed more than his shoulders, and Kenneth had to laugh. This was what he needed, distraction. His headache was lifting and that alone lifted his spirits.

"What were you telling your nephew? Dare I assume it was about me?"

Sir Richard leaned over and then bent down on his haunches. Others followed suit, as if they were about to hear a ghost story and they were surrounding a campfire.

Silence had to admit it caught his attention, and he sat on his haunches, too.

His friend's voice lowered and he took on the accent of a pirate, even squinting one eye as if he had a patch over it. "The night was heavy, and thick with humidity. Not a soul was comfortable in ter' breeches. No one could hide from what was t' come next. No one was safe. Each brother took the next in arms until a never-ending chain of honor was formed."

The crouching group all locked arms, and swayed rhythmically.

Sir Richard continued, "And we knew it the moment we saw him. We all understood our fate in that very moment. But we would not go down alone. We would fight it together. Brothers in arms! I am here to tell you, there is nothing more terrifying than seeing what has never been seen."

One of the younger gents blurted out, "What did you see?" He then sheepishly looked away as if he just showed his true colors.

"I's gettin' ther. Twas' not the darkness, nor the humidity, that brought the heaviness, but instead the night was thick with silence . . ."

The group all paused momentarily, waiting for the end. Finally Sir Richard repeated the last line with a bit of irritation, without the pirate's accent. "The night was thick with *Silence...*" His head bobbed up and down as if it would hammer it into the slow minds.

Then all at once the group toppled over, each linked together, and the cascade of laugher and enormous chuckles were shared universally. Kenneth hadn't realized just how "not himself" he had been, bringing the mood of the group down like a lead ball.

Silence hadn't been able to really let loose for a fortnight, and he was grateful for the invitation.

He spent the next hour completely ignoring any previous thoughts he had. No red curls, no lost station, no self-loathing of his "gift", and no irate father that he lost on the street.

He drank and laughed and shared his own jokes, none of which of the punch lines had to be repeated or hammered into the recipients.

He started to offer farewell bows and pounded Sir Richards on the back and said, "Thank you, sir. What pleasure I had in livening up the group." He winked.

"Aye, you did do that. But you were not ready when you joined! It was my pleasure to slap the silliness into you. But I must ask, one more; leave us with one more."

The group cheered and genuine compliments of how they enjoyed his company erupted. One even asked for a great one to bring home to his brother who was coming home from sea next week.

"Oh?" Silence asked. "Well, that does bring something I have been pondering of late. Pirates are known to have wooden legs, in fact it can make a pirate into a legend. Right? It is also considered a curse to have a woman on board. But what if, instead of wooden legs, women pirates had wooden breasts? That would be odd, wouldn't it?"

He let it sink in just half a second more, and said the last line with a slightly different emphasis, combining the sentence's words a bit. "It would be weird, wooden tit?"

As great a joke as he delivered, their reaction was far more entertaining.

That was why he lived the way he did.

When the way he lived made a life of joy for others, he felt he had a life worth living.

For the first time in weeks, nay, over a month, he went to bed without a thought about Miss Hughes.

*****

"My Lord, I cannot 'elp you. She's nowhere t' be found."

The Marquess of Tisdale's heart dropped. "Who else can we ask? There must be someone we have not utilized. Who will dig until satisfied? Until *I* am satisfied?"

Tisdale hated the northern accent, where they dropped all the H's, but he was running out of friends.

"There ain't no one else. You know that. 'onest, I have asked everyone, everyone except Silence, but you said you already asked 'im."

The marquess nodded. "Mmmm, yes, he had nothing to say."

"Per'aps you could ask yer mum to ask the ladyfolk."

"You numbskull, my mother has been dead for ages." Lord Tisdale was struck with a moment of longing for his mother.

"Do you have a lady friend?"

"*She* was my lady friend. I want her back! And time is of the essence."

He dismissed the street urchin and thought briefly, *Silence could find her; perhaps it is time I turn to him. He will just want to know why . . .*

*****

Evelyn turned towards the noise and saw the tall form of Eddie. Relief was a welcome friend.

"What are ye doin' out here at night, miss?"

She rarely even noticed his Irish brogue, but it seemed a bit strong tonight.

She lifted her nose and replied, "I should ask you the same thing. You should be at home with your wife and children."

He looked away briefly and readjusted his footing. "Aye, I was jus' checkin' the grounds one more time. Seems like things been goin' missin' lately. Been a bit nervous about leaving at night with no one here to protect ye both."

"Truly? I'm doubtful that was all you were doing. Do you attend us all night?"

She was marginally sure that he nodded, but when he bowed his head it was confirmed.

"Eddie, for what purpose?"

"Like I said, things been missin'. And there have been . . . noises."

She raised her eyebrow. "I do not catch your meaning. Did you also put the basket of food on the porch?"

"Aye. Tomorrow is market day, so I thought it would save ye the trouble."

Evelyn absorbed this new information and felt some relief from the mystery of things around her. But there was one thing that bothered her. The food, including meat, was left on the front doorstep. And Honeymae should have devoured it if she was outside with Eddie.

"Thank you. But is this where Honeymae has been? With you?"

His brow furrowed. "She isn't inside with ye both?"

She tried not to panic, taking a conscious breath before proceeding with her next statement. "I am sure she is sleeping in some corner, probably by the larder. It has been a bit hot tonight?" She hadn't meant to say it like a question but the thought was laced with doubt. Honeymae would have come if she were inside.

"Aye," he said flatly. She could tell he was scanning the perimeter of the cottage. He started slowly walking and she followed.

"Eddie, go home. You cannot protect us tomorrow when you have not slept."

"Nay, miss, I cannot. That is why I sleep outside." He motioned for her to look ahead.

They walked a bit more and turned towards the back of the cottage, and sure enough there was a horse blanket spread out on the side of the house, several feet from the neatly stacked wood pile.

She gasped. *Outside? He has been sleeping outside?*

She knew for certain that it had rained the night before, for most of the night. She turned back to him and planted her feet. "I cannot allow this. I shall not permit you to sleep on the ground for our sakes. It is totally unacceptable!"

"Ye might as well be whistling jigs to a milestone. Me mind is set."

The clouds moved just enough to see his Irish stubbornness at its finest in the moonlight. Although she felt some relief to know he would be around at night, she did not wish him to know that. "You are so stubborn."

She whistled one more time for Honeymae.

In the distance she heard her dog's paws pounding on the dirt.

She gave Eddie a worried look, then rightly scolded her dog for straying so far for so long. Honeymae was behaving strangely.

And they both knew it.

CHAPTER 7

Silence was close to ordering a third drink. The second was rare enough, but his head ached more than usual. From past history he knew a bit of cognac numbed the headache the best, but more than one drink also numbed his gift of discernment. And as much as this gift did not feel like a friend at the moment, he knew he never wanted to be without it entirely.

But the headache was horrid. It was not the typical ache when he knew someone was not being truthful. It was an internal ache, as if he himself was battling the truth.

It wasn't more than three hours ago that Miss Hughes' name came up unbidden.

One gentleman asked where she was.

Another asked why she never went to social functions.

Another replied that she was quiet, shy, and reserved.

The other said that he had heard she left the country to live as a hermit, and that she had always had secrets—an alternate life––and now she was exploring it.

That "alternate life" comment made good sport for the gentlemen in the party for over five minutes, as they speculated on what her secret life was.

The men brought up the less absurd first, like being an author, or dressing as a man to attend university. But when they said she was a witch, and was conjuring up a love potion with moon beams and turtle breath, he walked away. But only so far as to not disturb everyone by the pained look on his face.

The Miss Hughes that all of them knew was most definitely not a hermit, nor shy. And one of them had used the term, "awkward and peculiar." Miss Hughes, neither the one he learned to know back on the duke's land, or the one who entertained him in his sleep, could not be described this way.

Kenneth Silence had spent too much energy fighting the desire to think about Miss Evelyn Hughes during the day, but the fight ended when his head hit the pillow.

Almost without fail, he dreamed of her.

One dream in particular was a repeat of their battle of Shakespearian wits, one where the "payment" was to remove an article of clothing of the winner's choice.

He fondly remembered waking up to that dream the first time. In his mind, his very lonely dream-self had been far too practical in its choice of clothing article he desired to have her remove first.

The bonnet. He always hated her hideous bonnets.

But did he have to be such a gentleman in his dreams?

Shouldn't he be granted a bit of moral latitude when he was unconscious?

The memory had improved his mood a bit.

His head reminded him that his colleagues knew nothing of Miss Hughes.

They didn't know the fire in her eyes when she meant what she said, or the flirtatious tilt of her head when she didn't.

They didn't know that her quick mind seemed to grow quicker as his attraction grew. Or was it that *his* mind grew slower?

Either way, the headache was not because his friends had lied or attempted to mislead. The headache was because *both* parties were right. At least he felt they were.

And his gut, his knack for the truth, his innate talent, had never failed him or been wrong. The gentlemen all knew Miss Hughes to be shy and reserved. And he knew her to not to be. And he didn't understand it.

But he knew how he would. He felt a deep desire to return to the country.

*****

It had been two weeks since Mr. Phillip Thomas got the last letter, and he sorely missed his sweet Ester. He had been away

106

from her so long now that his hammock on deck would no longer conceal all the letters that he wished to take with him. They would be leaving port within a day or two, but for now, as his main duty was to monitor the loading and unloading of the cargo, he stored the letters in the hammock he slept in at dusk. He still couldn't say there was anything prettier than a sunset at the Falmouth coast.

"Sir, the last of the cargo be on the ship. The men'll be wantin' to know if they can be dismissed fer the last night."

"Yes, Jacobs, send them on their way." He folded the last letter and placed it on the hammock and turned to leave.

Jacobs was really Jacobson, but somehow it got shortened to Jacobs. He was a good lad; a bit thin, but a good lad.

"What were ye smiling about?"

He huffed a bit too forcefully. "I most certainly was not smiling."

"Well ye are now! Do ye have a lady? You are as straight and narrow as theys come!"

And before Phillip Thomas realized what was happening Jacobs had stepped past him and snatched the letter from his bunk, smelling it while he stepped towards the door. Looking down at the letter he said, "E. Hughes. Oooh, Miss Hughes, is it? Don't think she loves ya much 'cause it don't smell like girl's oils or nothin'."

Thomas' hand went immediately to the knife at his side, but when Jacobs noticed the game was surrendered, and the letter was back in the rightful owner's hand.

His heart pounded harder than it had for months.

Easy, Phillip; play it casual. Was he kidding himself? The man saw his reaction to protecting the letter. "Go. You saw nothing."

*****

It was such a pleasant moment.

Evelyn almost forgot her current circumstances. She sipped her tea and slyly took another fennel and lemon biscuit.

Grace kindly pretended not to see and asked, "I am quite sure that you have appreciated the drier weather recently."

"Indeed." She almost mentioned that laundry was easier to complete when there was no rain, but she didn't want to ruin the moment.

She felt like a lady again—a lady having tea with the Duchess of Huntsman.

"It made travel possible, I am sure." The duchess looked exquisite. Her hair was pulled back halfway, the front slightly falling to the same side as the rest, which was swept into a single, tempting, strawberry-blonde ringlet.

She had, of course, worn her best bonnet on the walk over. The blue one with silk flowers and pearls and a cascading yellow ribbon she had made a few months ago.

She momentarily admired the hat as it sat on the bench by the fireplace. And that made her think of Silence. She had come to believe he may be a better man than she thought. Truth was, she never thought he was bad, just interfering.

She redirected her thoughts because, as always, she was forced to remind herself that he had left.

By her own direction.

And, unexplainably, she missed him.

However, she reminded herself that this moment with her friend Grace, whom she had learned to adore, would not last forever. *Even if I want it to.* Tea with the duchess was an indulgence, and to not be fully engaged was preposterous.

She focused on her conversation with Grace, knowing that the afternoon sun would not last too much longer, perhaps another three hours, and she would need a bit of that time to get through the ravine. Without light, that trek could be disastrous.

Suddenly, Grace started to tell her about the first time she met Silence. Grace's ability to carry the moment in story was delightful. She had told Evelyn of the play on words she had used with his name, asking, "Must I stutter if I need you to stop talking? 'Silence, Silence.'"

Grace's laughter was less than ladylike, but far from unkind.

Her own laughter was therapeutic to both hear and experience. She had not laughed so easily since she had her verbal Shakespearian duel while folding laundry with Silence.

She had held back nothing in the duel, and this tempted Evelyn to share her own initial meeting of Kenneth Silence with the duchess. After all, the Halliburtons dinner party could be considered their first verbal duel.

After Evelyn finished, not leaving out the final cuts from both, Grace's jaw dropped. "You must be mistaken. There is no way he lit your music on fire on purpose, not with malintent."

"Oh yes, he did intend it, but I am beginning to doubt if it was with malice." In truth, she had doubted it for some time now.

They both startled a bit when the sitting room door opened and the butler came in and reported, "Mr. Kenneth Silence has called."

Evelyn's mind was wiped clean, entirely devoid of all thought.

She vaguely heard Grace state, in her regal duchess voice, "Splendid. Might you send him in with a bottle of his favorite sherry? I believe there might be an excellent year in the library."

Grace looked toward Evelyn and must have seen the panic written there. "On second thought, I believe I shall welcome him there in the library."

Bless you, Grace! Evelyn's spinning head began to slow, and she let out her breath.

But then she heard him.

She heard, not only his less-than-distant voice, but also his footsteps approaching the entrance to the sitting room, saying, "Nonsense, Gigi. The sitting room is fine."

*****

Silence was deeply fatigued from travel, but he was here, again, and passionately grateful that his headache had disappeared for the entire two-day voyage. With himself as his only companion in the carriage, his unique talent was easily put to rest. He was beginning to believe that solitude was the only cure for his headache.

Everyone else lied but himself.

He was struck with a thought. *Maybe that was why my great-grandfather changed his name from Sillians to Silence. Maybe he possessed the same talent, and just wanted silence.*

He redirected his thoughts to Grace Kingston, his best friend's wife. He kissed the hand she offered, but noticed it was stiffer than usual. Tense.

Her face looked strained, or nervous. He could not tell which. "Grace, how are you? Are you ill?" It was relieving to not have to assess the room, or other dangers here at Fleetwood Place. He trusted the duke and duchess, which usually put him at ease.

"Silence, Silence," Grace said impertinently, her eyebrow raised saucily, adding a smile. Then she added, "You, of all people, must know you should never ask, while greeting a lady, if she is ill. For it most definitely will be interpreted as saying, 'You look dreadful.'"

"Right you are. Let me make it up to you. What say you to a game of chess? I hear your king has only been taken once—by your husband, I believe."

The duchess seemed to jump at the opportunity, glancing towards the fireplace briefly for some unknown reason. "Yes; however, he only won because he distracted me. It was very bad of him." She reached her arm out to be escorted, and started walking towards the door even before he had taken it.

He forced the smile onto his face and asked, "Is the tea still warm?"

Grace Kingston blinked one too many times before answering. "Yes, warm but not hot. Let us request more as we commune in the library. The library is where we should go."

He tilted his head. "Why?"

"Why?" she parroted.

"Why must we go to the library?" he asked flatly. He looked around at the room once more, this time a bit more thoroughly. If he didn't know Grace so well, and her devotion to Gavin, he most definitely would have suspected she was entertaining someone. Someone she did not want Silence to know about.

He forced his eyes not to count the two teacups, but that would have been incongruent to his character and self.

He waited for her answer. He saw her awareness of the question in his eyes.

She inhaled briefly, exhaling a bit loudly. "I was entertaining."

He smiled and exhaled, too. "No, Grace, you *are* entertaining. I appreciate that you have kept the headache away a bit longer."

He bowed respectfully, then sat down.

She looked around, then reluctantly sat down as well.

It was then that he saw the hideous blue bonnet. The same one Evelyn wore when he somersaulted over Nimbus into the mud.

Suddenly he was no longer fatigued. He was instead stimulated, most persuasively.

He hardly heard Grace say that she was going to find her husband.

He was going to have tea with Miss Hughes.

*****

Evelyn attempted to hurry through the tunnel blindly. But soon realized she would not make it too far without injury. It would not do her, or Ester, any good if she broke her foot or slipped and hit her head.

She was struck with the horrid thought that no one would find her for days. Ester didn't know where the entrance to the caves was, even if she was able to descend the steep stairs to the bottom of the ravine, and most likely would never risk walking the three miles around the ravine and rocky cliffs. And Grace would have assumed she made it back to the cottage through the tunnel. Eddie would not have been alerted either because he had asked for one Sabbath a month off. That would mean he would arrive after dark and assume she was in the cottage.

She conceded that she must wait for Grace and Silence to leave the sitting room, to collect and light her lantern.

While she waited, hearing the distant murmurs through the false door, she let her mind drift.

Eddie had asked, repeatedly, all morning yesterday if Evelyn had used his ax.

Chopping firewood was one chore that she never attempted. Eddie was too proud to complain of the taxing labor, and his Irish temper would have melted her offending hands off with the heat of it if he saw her try to do such work. But it allowed her to practice her affronts.

She had said, with an exaggerated sniff in Eddie's direction, "Thou smell of mountain goat."

His temper started to retort, however he broke into laughter with his first word. "Aye, I do, miss. Now, which one was that from?"

"*Henry V*. But you are working so hard! You are like a dog who lost his bone. Now, here is a new one for you. You are an 'elvish-mark'd, abortive, rooting hog.'"

He swiped at his sweat-lined hat and pulled it to his middle as he laughed. When he caught his breath, he looked up and asked, "*Macbeth*?"

"*Richard III*. But really, Eddie." She sniffed at him again. "'Thou art unfit for any place but hell.'" She winked at him and offered, "Same play."

"Miss, I might butcher this 'cause it ain't one me ma read to me at Christmas." He cleared his throat, assumed the position of speechmaker, and added a dash of false poison, "Why don't you 'go to hell for a moment' . . . or such." His face contorted a bit in confusion. "I think it loses somethin' when I say it."

She giggled uncontrollably and said, "So close to completing it! The line is, 'go to hell for an eternal moment or so.'"

He winked at her and said, "Of course, for 'Merry wives . . .'" his chuckle escaped, he winked in preparation, and finished, "'. . . are the only ones who could deliver such an abuse so effectively.'"

She swatted at him with his own hat, then regretted it because her hands would smell of mountain goat for the rest of the day. She remembered thinking that if they had extra money this month, perhaps she would get him a new hat.

As she redirected her thoughts to listening through the false door to the sitting room, she realized that they no longer were talking. She waited several minutes before pressing her hand onto the mint painted wooden ring on the column, pressing it downward. The door gave way and it started to pivot, allowing a less than desired amount of space between the rotating pillar and the edge of the solid wall. She was a thin woman, but it required her to nearly hug the pillar and mince her feet around so that she ended up with her back to the sitting room.

She stepped away from the pillar only to reach for her bonnet, which was no longer on the bench by the fireplace.

She froze, hearing nothing but silence.

In that surreal moment, the deepest parts of her heart wished for one thing yet prayed for another. That was when she learned what her heart's strongest desires were.

She wanted Silence to be there.

CHAPTER 8

"Are you looking for something?" Silence attempted not to snicker. He had stashed the hat behind the chaise, just behind where he was sitting.

She looked like she had been caught; interestingly, not guilty-caught but embarrassed-caught. He felt a renewed appreciation for the strange gift he had.

How intriguing. Embarrassed, not guilty—yet caught nonetheless.

He felt his own draw deepen, and he stood.

Bowing, he said, "Miss Hughes."

She lifted her frozen stature enough to allow for an elegant curtsy, adding a saucy glance up at him from her feminine dip, maintaining eye contact as she returned to standing. "Good afternoon. What a pleasure it is to have you here at Fleetwood Place."

Her voice was exquisite, far better than he remembered.

Good Lord, Silence, who is embarrassed now?

"Ah, yes, I found that my mind needed to see the sights in Suffolk again."

"Your mind."

It had been said as a statement, not a question. So he did not answer. But he did say, "Do you come here often? Through a secret passageway?" He smiled, gesturing to the entrance she had just come through. He had once examined the pillars in this room, and they were identical. Except he had assumed that the pillar closest to the fireplace also had a moon at the top like all the rest.

She glanced back at the pillar and saw that it was still slightly ajar, and claimed, "I have. I do. I wish I could come more often, but my duties as mistress only allow for a visit once a week."

He suppressed the smile and probed, "How is it running your own estate?"

Evelyn began to walk away from him then looked over her shoulder at him, inviting him to join her.

He complied immediately; he was a gentleman after all. Something about her was different. She was more open, more flirtatious.

"I have been trained to be a mistress all of my life. I would say that even with all the training, I find there was much I was not prepared for."

"Truly? And what exactly was that?"

She smiled and said, "For one, the duties to entertain *unexpected guests,* delightfully of course."

He nodded and looked forward contemplatively, but his heart smiled. "Or knowing just the right way to send the obstinate ones on their way."

She cleared her throat when he glanced sideways at her. Her hand was fisted at her mouth, hiding her smile. He forced greater control of himself.

When she, too, had mastered herself again, Evelyn added, "Nor was I experienced enough to know how to apologize. Ladies of society are taught to never surrender, unless it is their . . ."

". . . honest opinion."

She released an adorable laugh in agreement. "Most definitely. That is, until you marry. The lady is then allowed to reveal the unpleasantness she had learned to hide in order to ensnare a husband. By then . . ."

"Those poor, weak saps," he said while bowing his head. "They have no idea until they wake up to someone who is nothing more than a painted lady."

"Perhaps that is why they say we use their our 'arts and allurements' to find a good match."

They both laughed and turned towards each other.

Evelyn spoke first, slowly. "I am truly sorry. I did not mean to have called you ungentlemanly months ago. I now believe that you might have been trying to spare me public shame when you prevented me from singing."

She spoke with such measured intensity.

It was raw, and real. It was honest.

The honesty broke down his reserve, and he felt his eyes gloss over.

He took a calming breath and hushed the words. "I had no other intent."

"I now am fully aware." Her exhale had a flirty feminine quality, if that was even possible.

The relief washed over him. He hadn't realized how much it bothered him that she felt he was an "arrogant, interfering fool". His life was devoted to being honest, and those who knew him really liked him because he did not pretend like the rest.

"I, too, must apologize. I had made judgments about you that night, too. I usually am not so blind." He turned to her, grabbing her hand in both of his. "But now I see there is a depth to you that I have the greatest desire to explore. A strength I must attempt to comprehend. A soul that is kind and generous. Your mind is quick and sharp, yet you have a heart that has a softness that I cannot grasp yet. It has known so much sorrow and pain; pain I hope to help heal. I would be a fool if I allow myself to walk away from what I see as nothing short of extraordinary."

She looked at him, her lips slightly parted. Her eyes had novels to say, yet she said none of it. He stepped a bit closer. Her eyes widened a bit, but there was no fear.

There was hope.

*****

As she looked up at his handsome face, which carried a good day's stubble from travel, she knew she could not speak.

He stepped even closer and Evelyn felt him let out his breath a bit, making her pull hers in. His breath was sweet, and warm. She tilted her head up to smell more of it.

Evelyn did not know she had closed her eyes; the moment was playing out in her head so well without needing to see it happen.

Kenneth Silence's lips feathered the corner of hers and she turned into them gratefully, nay, eagerly.

His lips were gentle, but full of restraint. She solicited her toes to lift her body to better fit his arms, which had gathered her at the small of the back and her neck.

It was not a sacrifice, and the return was worth the invested effort.

With his chest against hers she no longer just smelled his breath, or tasted it. It was more than that. As his passion increased, she felt the very movement of his chest as he pulled her into the kiss. It was like he was actually breathing her in; taking a part of her soul that she knew she wouldn't have given, at least not willingly, six or seven months ago.

But she was feeling generous this afternoon. So she gave all she could to Silence with her own kiss.

She was suddenly struck with the thought that her father would be appalled.

She could hear him now. *"What will people say? Tell me you have discussed his finances before you tossed your future, dowry, and reputation to a third son like cracked corn to a pigeon. This cannot be undone, but I will try anyway."*

She accidently let out a giggle, which only generated more.

She took a step back and was able to squeak out, "For-forgive me-ee-ee. I just was . . ." she released a hearty laugh, then blurted the rest out, ". . . thinking about my father!" She continued to laugh, then had to look for her handkerchief. She was sure she looked quite undignified.

She finally found her handkerchief then turned to find equal parts confusion, incredulity, and pure amusement on Silence's face.

Perhaps a bit more amusement than the others, she thought.

His eyebrow rose, quirked his head a bit, and asked, "While we were kissing . . . you thought of your father?. We were . . . well, *I* was having the greatest moment of *my* life!" He pretended to bow his head in shame.

He was too easy to read. She did not answer him because she knew he was not affronted. Instead she put her hand on her hip, cocked it, and said, "Well, perhaps your kisses were not up to my expectations."

Glancing up, he cleared his throat, suddenly standing erect and far less playful.

Had she offended him? Surely he knew she was joking. But then she followed his gaze.

She turned around to find the duke, with his wife on his arm, as still as statues. Both were staring at them, as if it would change the hush in the room that had just materialized into something tangible.

Then Gavin looked at his wife and said, "I thought they were mortal enemies."

Later that evening, Evelyn pondered how Grace was able to say it with a straight face. "Well, dear, they are mortals. Perhaps they are trying to keep their friends close and their enemies closer."

"Yes, I believe you are right, dear. They must be the worst of enemies, for they were holding each other very close."

*****

"I am so glad you are staying for dinner," Grace admitted while she fastened the last of the buttons on the gown Evelyn was borrowing from Grace. Of course she had brought no eveningwear to Fleetwood Place, but neither was there any at the cottage.

"Please thank Cook for having it prepared early enough for me to be able to return home while there is still daylight."

Evelyn could see Grace's face in the mirror. She had closed her mouth, as if she were biting her tongue.

"Grace?" Evelyn felt remorse for making it sound like a chastisement the second time. "Grace? What is it?"

Her only reply was, "Hmmmm?" without even looking at Evelyn in the mirror.

"I cannot claim to know you well, but I do know you well enough to know that you rarely hide your opinion."

Her hands paused in motion. "You just called the cottage 'home'. Do you really feel that way?"

"I did? Oh my, I suppose I did. I have lived there now for about six months. Or has it been longer?"

"Since the New Year, my dear. You were sent here two weeks after . . ."

She sighed. Yes, she remembered. Two weeks after the Halliburtons' dinner party. It was mid-July now. "So, seven months? More than half a year." *I was to be paraded on every eligible bachelor's arm all throughout the finest places of London. My, how dreams can change.*

"Oh! I have splendid news! Phillip found work as an assistant to the captain. He is being mentored to replace the captain."

"Speaking of whom, how is Ester?"

"Splendid. I believe she is struggling with sleep, though. Too many times now I have found her out of her bed, or Honeymae left outside."

"I can imagine. This would be such a hard time, with all the strain and stress of your circumstances, to not have Phillip. And time does not stop turning or speed up, even if she wishes for it."

"I am so anxious to hear if Mother and Father have finally made it safe to return."

Grace finished with the last button, and said, "After the sitting-room incident, Gavin and I had a moment to ourselves while you were refreshing. We do not often completely agree on much, but we most definitely agreed on this. We think you should hire Silence to help your mother and father. You have spent enough time there in the cottage."

"Oh, no. I cannot do that. I hardly know the man!"

Grace smiled and raised her eyebrow.

"Well, I let him kiss me, but that does not mean he should know why we are out here. Besides, I cannot pay him. It would go against Father's rules. 'No servants except for Eddie. No horses. No carriages. No socializing.' None of it."

She felt a cold chill run down her spine as she repeated the rules. She could almost see his solicitor's handwriting, spelling out his tone of voice as he ordered him to write the demands.

Of course, she hadn't been there, nor actually heard her father state the rules, but she had heard her father speak in such a matter on many occasions. The instructions had come by way of a letter that her mother presented to them. It was too easy to conjure it in her mind, though.

"Perhaps you should not dismiss the idea altogether. But I know you well enough, too, to know your pride would never let you ask Silence for help."

Both ladies knew, without further retort, that the conversation was over.

She wasn't prideful, was she? Not anymore.

CHAPTER 9

Gavin handed Kenneth Silence the lit lantern. He put a hand on his shoulder, and nodded.

Kenneth couldn't help but hear the concern in his own voice as he said, "We should not have enjoyed ourselves at dinner so long. I am unfamiliar with the journey, or how long it takes. It was irresponsible of me."

"Nonsense. It only takes about ten minutes if you are in a hurry." He winked, then added, "Twenty-five if you are enjoying yourself. It is about a mile walk. Not a bad shortcut."

"Most definitely. Going around the ravine is more than a three-mile ride, and a bit of a brutal one at that."

"That is because a horse cannot fit through the tunnel, nor climb the three flights of steps out of the ravine. But I will tell you that it beats going around the out-jutting of rocky cliffs." Gavin looked out the sitting-room window and said, "You might want to leave now, if your goal is to enjoy yourself. I doubt you have much more than forty minutes until you, too, must be back down the ravine before the sun has completely set."

Silence nodded his agreement and walked the few step to fetch the lady he was escorting. "Miss Hughes."

She took his offered arm, until it was time to fit through the narrow space and mince around the rotating pillar.

It was not difficult for either of them, but it *was* awkward.

Which basically summed up the first five minutes of the walk through the cave. So much was communicated without a word spoken.

It was a bit damp, and there was the rare puddle to navigate around. Most of the time the path was wide enough for them to walk side by side, which he preferred since there was only one lantern. That was his fault. He had declined a second lantern because he did not wish her to have to carry one, and he wouldn't give up the opportunity to have her on his remaining arm.

If he was honest, he almost hoped she might have a fright and seek comfort in both of his arms.

What am I saying? I am always honest!

Miss Hughes had been on his mind for about six weeks. There were so many questions that he desperately wanted to ask. He had gained information that seemed to be obtained without actively seeking it out.

And he had tried very hard not to seek information about her.

"May I ask a question?" she asked, her voice soft and a bit timid.

Was she afraid?

"Of course," he responded casually.

He had sensed that the last few minutes of walking in general silence was because they each held thoughts, albeit probably on different topics, that they did not wish to talk about.

"What has society been told about me leaving, and do they believe it?"

A chuckle with a bit of a cough escaped. He loved her honesty! What woman broaches the most difficult topic first, without so much of a mincing of words?

"Well, there are a few working theories. I will tell you I never sought information because I am the kind of gentleman who prefers to get the information right from the source. But your name did come up a few times. The numerous rumors fell at my feet from everyone but you." He chanced a glance sideways and barely caught her withdraw bravely, with a deep breath.

He continued. "Be assured, I will not ask what the truth is. But it does not mean I do not dearly wish to know. One theory is that you are an author, of the less-than-respectable form of novels."

She gasped. "You jest with me!"

"No, no, I do not. But I wanted to break the ice with something quite shocking. The only one that might have had any merit was that your extended family was in need of assistance somewhere. The other theories are not so deranged. Unless you have a very passionate side of you, more passionate than what you have already shown me . . ." he said, wiggling his eyebrows playfully.

"If you tease me so, I shall show you just how passionate I can be at boxing your ears. You are supposed to be my escort!"

"True, and I admit I am not that great of an escort, but I gather it is more escort than you have had in, what, six or more months?"

The light from the lantern had caught the slightest nod.

She then diverted that comment momentarily as she asked, "What other theories are the elite spreading about my disappearance?"

"Well, my favorite, and the most logical, is that you are a witch."

A single gasp from Evelyn was the best reward, but he pressed on with the rumor. "And that you are making a love potion using a thousand-year-old recipe—including moonbeams and turtle breath." He stopped walking momentarily and turned to her.

She had a delightful smile on her face. "It is a full moon— perfect for harvesting moonbeams."

He was pleased she saw the humor of it. "Pardon me, but how long does the love potion take?"

"Oh, a great deal longer than you think,"

"How long has it truly been?"

She seemed to suck in a breath and hold it for an immense amount of time.

"It has been six months, nearly seven." The previous guarded breath was released, and the rest of her body released as well. First it was her head, then shoulders, then the chest seemed to deflate, and yet somehow each step appeared painful to take.

They were making too much progress. At least, he thought so.

"Miss Hughes." He stopped and waited for her to stop and turn, too. She turned, but he waited a moment longer until she lifted the chin to look at him. "Miss Hughes, come here."

He placed the lantern on the ground, raised his arms up halfway, in front of him, and waited.

There was a darkness that could not be described in seeing her shoulders sag so morosely.

When she lifted her eyes, it was only enough to see fear—complete terror—of what she would be told next.

"Come. Just pretend that I am whoever you need me to be." His outstretched arms beckoning. "Brother, father, friend, whomever."

She hesitated, not once but twice. Then the hesitation fled.

He took the same single step forward as she did, and wrapped his arms around her. One arm wrapped naturally around her shoulder, his hand landing at her tiny waist. The other cradled her head to his chest.

She had come at him with her hands at her face, blindly, not just from tears but because she had covered her face so shamefully.

What on earth has happened to this woman? How could a soul hurt and suffer as she clearly had been, with parents in London who had both the means and upbringing to treat her the way she deserved?

Where was the lady who delivered her gloriously saucy retorts with more spice and pizazz then Shakespeare ever intended? What weighty conditions could make these tiny but proud shoulders ever feel this heavy?

"What . . ." He began to ask these questions, but then thought better. "What can I do? Ask me, and it is yours."

There was a minimal shift; however, she didn't push away except to move the hands that had still been covering her face. "I believe you just did."

Unprepared for her to meet his unspoken desire she moved her arms, hesitantly, around his back and pressed her cheek to his chest, relaxing into his form. Her warm breath crossed over his chest as if he had just drunk something warm.

It tingled, but from the inside out; a sensation he had never had except when he had a sure knowledge that someone was telling the truth.

But she had said nothing.

Whatever just happened to him was familiar, and instinctive, and oh so honest.

CHAPTER 10

The light of late dusk was not much, however it was far more than what was in the cave. The narrowness of the ravine made it feel even later. But she knew they were not far now.

Risks of the heart were dropping like flies on frosted shortbread. The conversation had tended to be fairly light the rest of the way out of the cave, and even out into the sunlit ravine.

As he spoke, she wondered how a man's voice could sound cool and warm at the same time. Cool because it was refreshing, and seemed to soothe the heat in her heart. But warm also because the larger part of her mind had turned cold, almost lifeless— lacking conversation and interaction with her peers.

His cool, soothing voice cracked, but just slightly. "I have shared with you what others say, but may I ask why you left society? Or, more importantly, why you stayed away? I understood that after the Halliburtons dinner party you admitted no visitors, not even the Marquess of Tisdale. I also understand that there was an underst—"

"No. There was not." Her heart fluttered a bit, although not as much as she expected in hearing her former suitor's name. She rationalized the fluttering was because her mind was brought back to that traumatizing night. The party itself was fine. It was what came afterwards.

She sighed, then sighed again. Looking in his eyes boldly, even pleadingly. "That night seemed to last forever, even lasting until today. Like the sun never really set."

She stopped herself and quickly looked away. *You cannot tell him!*

"I would not know, as I left shortly after being called an arrogant, interfering fool."

She let out a genuine laugh, although short-lived.

"See here, Evelyn," he said, "You have sighed more than I have heard oxen huff when pulling quartz out of a quarry. Just breathe. Normally. Do it with me. In normally, but exhale two times longer."

Looking away she pondered what to say, but practiced the breathing; more to be polite than anything else.

Could she—*should* she—share with him what happened?

How she would love to confide in someone other than those who already knew. Her eyes immediately flooded, and she blinked the tears determinedly away.

They had walked the short fifty meters between the cave's entrance and the foot of the three flights of rickety steps that allowed them to climb out of the ravine. Staring up at the steps, she felt determined reason bubble up inside again and said, "I should like to trust you a bit more first."

"I see."

She started the climb, knowing their conversation, this conversation, would be greatly hindered due to the climb, especially the pace she was choosing. "I admit that I trust you more than I normally trust other men."

"Ideally one trusts the *men* they kiss." The emphasis was unmistakable, but teasing nonetheless.

Her head snapped around in shock, but even confirming his wide, teasing grin did not hold back her retort. "*Men*? You think I have kissed *multiple* men?" She felt the teensiest bit of the old fire of hatred and indignation from being judged differently than she was.

He doused it easily because his only answer was a single eyebrow that rose at a snail's pace. When that lone brow rose to its highest the other joined in a playful, and very flirtatious, wide-eyed dance.

Her once-affronted thoughts were lost in his playfulness and the genuine kindness of his hazel eyes. He then stepped up and kissed her again. With him on a step lower, their faces melted together effortlessly.

She decided that was not the best method of getting the upper hand, because shortly thereafter she was forced to collect herself. "*Hrrumph*," she murmured, and turned back to climbing.

After passing the midway point she could hear his breath a bit hitched, but she pressed on further, leaving no doubt that she did not intend to stop for a rest. Perhaps the honest thing was that she was better at hiding her breathlessness. She had climbed these steps plenty of times, so she focused her energy in the climb. *"Show no weaknesses. At least not to him."*

"Pardon?" he said breathily.

She froze, and slowly turned towards him, a few steps below her stopping point. She had done it again: said her thoughts out loud.

He must have seen her panicked face.

"Is there something amiss?" He caught up to her, only two steps below her. His face was slightly lower than hers. He asked again, "Who were you talking about? You said, 'Show no weaknesses, at least not to him.' Who? Is there a man who is harming . . ."

Evelyn saw him get more concerned, almost protective, glancing above them, then around them.

He had no idea that she accidently said what she was thinking out loud about showing no weakness to him, Silence.

He gently guided her panicked body to the side and cautiously started the climb, this time as the leader.

Honeymae welcomed him with a three-bark warning, putting her a bit more at ease.

With Evelyn's nerves momentarily on fire, she was reminded of just how intimidating her English Mastiff could be.

It was an interesting next ten minutes as he transformed in front of her from the funny, intelligent man she had been getting to know, the same man she once thought was obstinate and intrusive, into a gentleman who was entirely devoted to her safety. His eyes never stopped absorbing and processing what was around them.

After walking around the cottage, with him on full alert, she jested, "Are you satisfied?"

He was still looking around suspiciously, guardedly. "Who planted the garden? It looks like it will have maximum yield. How much male assistance did you have?" His words were slightly forced, like he was trying to make small talk but didn't know how to do it.

She answered him honestly. And since he was staring at the slightly irregular rows of the oat field, she stated, "I did. I sowed my oats wild."

He coughed and then grinned. "I believe the saying is 'I sowed my wild oats."

She raised her eyebrow. "I do not think that is correct."

He chuckled joyfully. "I am afraid that is how you say the phrase. But even if I am mistaken, do you know what that particular idiom means?"

"It means I planted oat seeds in the wild, or in a wild way."

She could not believe he belly laughed at her comment, and more than once! It was like he could not stop!

"I beg your pardon, sir, but what exactly is so funny?"

Between near-coughs and chuckles, he stated, "Naivety is so becoming of you, my dear. But, 'sowing your wild oats' means you are generous with your favors." He cleared his throat twice before saying, "It is generally said about bachelor men who know a great many ladies."

Her blush started from somewhere in her body, but it mattered not because it ended up *everywhere*. There would be no hiding the flush's presence from her gentleman escort.

Evelyn! What is wrong with you? Even that, *sounded inappropriate!*

She had nothing to say, for the thoughts she had could not to be shared.

For the entire time he was laughing at her embarrassment, which was more than a minute or two, her mind searched for anything at all to say.

The only thing that came out was Shakespeare.

"'Go hang yourself.'" The words from *Troilus and Cressida* seemed to fit perfectly.

He paused in his laughing enough to deliver a marvelous smile and retort, softening her fury. "Really, so harsh a retort, an abuse of the worst kind. From one whose 'hard heart is buttoned up with steel . . .'"

"You, you . . . you dare use *Comedy of Errors* prose on me? Did you fail to remember the next line? Let me help you. ' . . . buttoned up with steel, pitiless and rough.'"

"I did not fail to finish it at all. In my mind, the rest of the line did not apply to you. You are neither pitiless, nor rough."

Her mind was quickly thinking up the next reply, and failed to absorb what he meant. She artfully delivered the next line with passion, although it surprised her that her own words were already laced with humor, and possibly a bit of lure. "'The villainy you teach me, I will execute, and it shall go hard, but I will better the instruction.'"

His smile softened slightly, and he turned his head slightly in doubt.

She did the same thing, but more in challenge, tilting the chin subtly.

He narrowed his eyes, which hadn't lost a bit of the energy from laughing. He closed his lips in false sternness, but the mirth was still apparent.

Evelyn couldn't help but minimally appreciate how it made him look handsome and regal. Perhaps it was more than *minimally*. It was the hazel eyes that never stopped smiling. Or was it the day's dark stubble on the strong jaw? But neither one of those was nearly as intriguing as the way his waistcoat fit.

She collected herself, then briefly chided herself for needing collecting at all.

At least he hadn't noticed, for when he still hadn't responded she chose to maximize the opportunity to come off as conqueror. She delivered one of her favorites from *The Tempest*.

Patting her dog's head, she said, "'He is winding up the watch of his wit, by and by it will strike.' Honeymae, do you suppose he knows he will lose again?"

"Again? You are mistaken, madam. I have never lost to you." Then, in a quieter voice, he said, "Surrender is another story." He smiled and continued, "But nevertheless, I shall watch my back in a spar with you, for 'a friend like thee might bear my soul to hell.'"

He was laying on the charm, a bit thick, too, and yet it was not unwelcomed. He exhaled, as if it was over, as if he was surrendering already, but she was not ready for it to end. The competition, the fight, the drive to conquer, was invigorating on so many levels.

"'O faithless coward . . .'" She was sure he would not be familiar with *Measure for Measure.*

But he was. "'O dishonest wretch.'"

She gasped in both surprise and intrigue, but quickly closed her mouth again. How refreshing to feel the energy and charisma of the moment tickle her spine in excitement. She hadn't felt this alive in some time.

She gave him the harshest look she could muster, but could not hide the merriment. She may have felt her hips sway with a mind of their own, which was the greatest disappointment. She frowned in frustration.

Another chuckle escaped, then he stifled it with a terrible but incorrect addition to the conversation from *Coriolanus*, "'The tartness of' *her* 'face sours ripe grapes'."

"It is '*his* face sours ripe grapes'. You are a 'fellow of no mark, nor likelihood' Kenneth."

He blinked suddenly, momentarily startled; his face became serious for moment, as if the game had ended or his mind left momentarily. He shook his head as if he was trying to refocus.

"Is there something wrong? Silence? I did not mean it, any of it, of course. I perceived this was just another diversion."

"You used . . . no, it was nothing. I did not know you knew my name."

"Silence?"

"Kenneth, Kenneth Silence."

"Of course I know your name. 'Thou hast no more brain than I have in my elbows.'" She assumed since the verbal duel had started with *Troilus and Cressida*, she should end with it as well.

Apparently he was not one to let it end, though. He took a gentle step closer and reached a hand towards her chin. The words of riposte sounded more like a caress, as he said softly and tenderly, "'Chide God for making you the countenance you are.'"

Of course he kissed her silent.

She blinked, looked away and swallowed hard, hoping the new flush was not apparent.

How is it she actually felt flattered with the way he quoted Shakespeare's well-known affront?

Finding her voice, she said, "Perhaps you should return to Fleetwood Place."

"Yes, perhaps so." But he made no effort to do so.

In order to get him to leave before the sun completely disappeared, she finally stated that everything around the cottage looked in order. And that she had no fear that anything was amiss.

He nodded, clearly not satisfied. But at least satisfied enough to return to the rickety stairs near the ravine.

She shadowed him to the ravine, without words, and the reason she followed was simply not important to her at the moment. She was content to do what felt good. And silence felt good.

He turned and pressed, "Tomorrow—can I see you tomorrow?"

She smiled, but agreed to *sacrifice* a visit at tea tomorrow in order for him to be satisfied.

Perhaps some sacrifices could be more appreciated than the others of late.

She giggled. And, oh, how good it felt.

CHAPTER 11

Evelyn Hughes felt the evening had more calmness to it than she had felt for a lengthy period. Somehow things felt more settled, less transient. It was as if her feet were solidly planted on the ground, and that it had stopped shaking. But it was more than that.

She knew enough of what was expected of her when she chose to come here with her sister. She would be doing more than a gently bred lady was trained to do, or should do for that matter. The shock of the daily fatigue was overwhelming. Oh, the physical work was hard, but that was not what usually left her exhausted.

The utter surrender to the bed every night was caused from feeling like she had to protect her sister and herself. She felt that, should anything happen, it would be from her oversight.

It was unlikely she would ever say it to Ester, but her mind was usually going over the list of things that needed to be done, prioritizing them, and racing to check them off daily. There was no question that the majority were chores and tasks that only she could do. Ester helped with dishes and keeping the floor swept, and would always make the beds, set the tea out, and even help fold the dried laundry on a good day.

But Evelyn didn't feel that reoccurring list running right now.

Instead she thought about Kenneth Silence.

The kisses were indeed pleasant, and his company was a salve to her lonely soul.

Although his flirtations were laced with Shakespeare's words, they still felt honest and sincere.

No, tonight's peace was from none of that.

It was his determination that she must not walk home through the cave alone, offering himself as escort. It was his voiced concern while in the cave, that he did not want her to misstep. No one had worried about her lately.

Then, after misinterpreting the fear in her eyes at the top of the stairs from the caves and ravine, he chivalrously went first, knowing nothing at all of what dangers lay ahead. Which, of course, was nothing at all.

He appeared to be on full alert after that, indicated by his careful checking of the cottage prior to leaving. She shared that Eddie did not sleep at the cottage, not usually. He did interrogate her briefly but then just absorbed what she had said, as if weighing it carefully, like a miser pinching his pennies.

He knew what it all meant. He knew the sacrifices she had been through. And yet it was more than that, too.

It was his perceptive eyes that took in her circumstances, followed by him stooping to place the few fallen firewood bundles and stacking them while they talked, saying, "You would not wish to trip in the night."

It was his eyebrow raised in concern, concern for her when the sun went down, speaking volumes but saying none of it.

And she could not deny it was his praise that made her shiver in the warmth of the sunset. *"You manage well, disconcertingly well, by yourself,"* somehow validated the work she had done daily for almost seven months.

Dusk had come and gone over thirty minutes ago, sending Mr. Silence down the rickety stairs. But not before he vowed to secure the top step better the next day, instructing, "Please refrain from using it until I may have a chance to do so."

She exhaled, and then smiled. This, this she would concede in.

All in all, she didn't know how else to quantify or qualify what she felt other than this.

She felt safe.

*****

Evelyn woke up again to a noise. Scratching?

"Honeymae, *shhhh* . . ." she whispered, lazily scanning the darkness to see if her dog had woken her sister.

Ester mumbled sleepily, "She wanted to be let out a while ago. She probably wishes to come back in."

Her sister sounded so tired. She should have been the one to let her dog out. How did she not hear her beast of a dog whining at the door? An English Mastiff does not have a quiet whine. She felt rested enough to investigate. It was half past three in the morning.

One slipper was not sliding on as well as the other and she stooped to assist the back, pausing as something other than scratching alerted her suddenly.

Smoke.

It was late July and no one used fires at night. She preferred a single bed sheet unless she'd had too much sun that day, but usually hardly even a lap blanket.

Her heart started beating a bit faster, confusion swirling in her mind. Urgency convinced her that her slipper would have to do as is—bent under the heel.

Picking up the pace, she scanned the predawn darkness. Fire of any form right now was not welcome. It had been unusually warm and dry for this part of England for several weeks. She imagined some rider tossing his cigar carelessly along the road.

But the smoke was not on the horizon. It was closer than she was comfortable with.

Turning around she forced herself to search the premises, but did not go far when her slipper stuck in the mud from where they dumped the dishwater out the window that night.

"Well, it was of no use anyway," she mumbled. "And my fault for not carrying the water further from the house."

She pushed further, turned the corner towards the back of the cottage, and learned what she had thought was scratching was not.

The fire ablaze on the woodpile drew her entire attention, spitting and crackling, as if in competition with the angry hissing of the wood.

"Fire! Ester, wake up! Fire!" she called over her shoulder at the open cottage door. She started running towards the fire, looking one way and then the next for something to drench it with.

Eddie's blankets!

She dashed to the left briefly and tripped on something very big, landing half of her body on the offending mass, and her face into a foul-smelling work hat she knew too well from the day of plowing.

"Eddie!"

She scrambled around, shaking him, his left side of his face smashed sideways in the dirt, with two dribbles of blood glistening with the light from the fire rolling off his right side of his head. He was over eight feet from the fire, but still too close.

She grabbed one of Eddie's boots and tried to pull him further away. She moved him only inches, when she realized his face was dragging in the dirt and rocks.

She shook him again and yelled his name, panic starting to take control.

Pain wakes anyone up, she decided, and she had not enough time to think of another plan. "You get up this instant. I cannot move you. Now do as I say." She put her hands on her hips and gave him a good kick in the knee.

He did not move much, but groaned adequately.

She fell to her knees, trying to see through her tears. "That is right, sir, now is not a good time for you to be slacking in your duties."

He grumbled something.

"Speak up! Get up. Do anything. This cannot be happening." She glanced at the fire, but there was no need to have looked. Its heat was becoming more intense.

She was determined to have nothing happen to Eddie or her sister. Even though Eddie was lean, he was one of the tallest men she knew. Because of that, his mass was greater than she could move. She attempted to roll him over, assuming that if his legs turned the hips would follow, then chest and eventually the rest of his person. It was a good guess.

Luckily, in the process he yelled out when the final flop finished. "Where, ehh, my head. Where is he?"

"Eddie, please get up. I have to get my sister out. The cottage is on fire."

"Didn't see 'em . . ."

"Get up!"

He looked up groggily and then seemed to absorb the intense heat; he scrambled to his feet, unnaturally wobbly. She slid under his arm and helped him, but the speed was not what she wished it. Her heart was battling between helping him further or leaving him to rescue Ester.

The decision was made for her. Suddenly Eddie's weight was relieved of her and he let go, but it was not of his own accord.

Kenneth Silence had taken the other side and was escorting him away. She ducked out from under the arm and ran into the cottage. The smoke was billowing inside as the back of the cottage, likely the storage room, was alit.

"Ester, wake up!" She knew the cottage well, but did not gauge the distance from the front door to her sister's bed well and her slipper-less foot found the leg of the bed first.

She shrieked, letting the dizziness from the pain consume her momentarily. Her breath was labored, and it was only then that she realized she should be covering her mouth. Her lungs burned as she shook Ester.

Luckily it did not take long before her sister understood what was going on, and with Evelyn's help got up awkwardly and headed towards the door.

That darn slipper-less foot stepped on Honeymae's well-chewed-up bone, causing it to pierce the skin.

Before she could take her dog's name in vain, she remembered she had not yet found her. "Honeymae! Come!" Her eyes darted every which way, hoping to see her, but the smoke was terribly thick.

A male voice said, "Here, come here."

It was Kenneth Silence. Her eyes burned and she followed, trying to convince herself that Honeymae was let out earlier.

Please, God, save my dog. She stumbled the last five feet towards the door, looking out into the distance, hoping to see her pounding towards her to save them all with her fawn and black brindled mass of fur and wrinkles.

"Did she get out?" she whimpered in a scratchy voice, not realizing that she did not own her breath. She took another labored breath and asked at the exact moment that Kenneth Silence scooped her up just inside the threshold, briskly turned sideways, and exited the cottage. Making quick progress away from the place she had called home. "Did she get out?" Evelyn coughed hard, sounding coarse, and more like a bark.

There was a bit of silence, then he said while walking away briskly, "Yes, your beast got out. She has been howling for the last ten minutes."

Confusion hit her in equal portions of offense and disgust. "Do not call my sister a beast. She is with child." She wanted to reprimand him further but her restricted, smoke-filled lungs would not let her.

"Sister?" he asked.

That single word, saturated with concern and confusion, completely undid her.

No! No! No! No! She squirmed and wrestled to be put down, and once he complied she dashed back towards to cottage. "Ester! Ester!"

"Miss Hughes, stop! The roof is on fire. Do not go back in!"

She was running. Even though she hadn't the strength, she pushed through the fatigue. The door had blown shut again, or had Silence shut it?

She threw her weight at it but it opened easier than usual, and there was Ester, tightly carrying the fishing basket of letters from her husband, Phillip. They must have been opening the door at the same time.

Tears were running down their faces as they hugged tightly. Relief flooded her person and they were escorted by both Eddie and Silence, away from the wood-shingled roof that was falling piece by piece.

Both ladies were coughing, or barking fairly regularly, but they were going to survive.

The men were checking them over for injuries while the ladies sat and watched as their home for the last seven months fell in front of them.

It was such a small cottage that a fire simply took it to its grave. The men knew it, too, or they would have been trying to drench it. They all knew that anything that was in it would be ruined.

Her dog was lost, but now found, Eddie had hit his head somehow, and Ester almost died going back inside to get her letters, her home was demolished, and yet she was perfectly at ease having Silence assess her so indiscriminately.

Mr. Silence's thorough appraisal of her person should have shocked her, or at least degraded her, but it did not. He had gratefully wrapped his coat around her nightclothes, but only after he had assured that no major injury had occurred on her arms, and she assumed he had checked her back.

No, she wasn't injured. Not really. She had lost so much. She should be examining her dog who somehow had found them and was now lapping at the abrasions on knees.

Or maybe she should be worried about her sister. But she felt nothing right now. Not even gratitude in being alive.

She should have inquired how Eddie was doing.

At least be grateful for something, she instructed herself. The wind felt cool on her heated skin. She would be grateful that the sun was making its presence known behind her.

But it felt forced.

No, she couldn't. Her spirit could not do it. There was nothing left inside. The numbness was wearing off, and she sensed an impending loss of control as her knees started knocking together uncontrollably.

She knew she couldn't reach the level of refinement she was demanding of herself at the moment. To find gratitude at a time of loss. She had failed in everything she had promised her father she would become.

She could hear him now. *"Being a lady of society takes refinement and being in control at all times."* Her spine felt weaker by the minute, and her chin was no longer parallel to the ground. Yes, things were slipping. And very quickly, too.

Her father would have plenty to say if he saw her. *"If you must have emotion, do not show it in front of me or any of our peers. The ton's eyes always remember. Bring shame to yourself in private. I will have none of it."*

But the wee hours of this particular morning he would have said, *"You are an adult, now act like one. Your tears have failed me."*

Her father would be mortified.

The social theatrical game had been lost moments ago.

So, she simply stopped suppressing the sobbing that was maddening to suppress.

No need to be ladylike now.

*****

At least he had not found any blood or raw, burned skin. His breathing had been hitched as he diligently searched her person. Kenneth's assessment had made it to her feet, when he thought he saw her flinch and his heart dropped.

But when he looked up at her, her flinch was not from physical pain. Even through the reflection of the fire, he saw a depth in her distant hazel eyes as deep as the caves he toured on the Falmouth coast. But raging wild, like the rocky coast at Lyme Regis.

He just watched her stare ahead as if he was not there. The brows almost spoke for themselves of the pain she felt, the sorrow written across her bosom, which was repeatedly caving with each breath. Yet her arms just shook limp from the sobs. Her strong but feminine jaw-line, that he had once greatly admired, had lost its natural angles as her mouth gracefully moved with the crying.

He took a breath, then two. He was not one to feel helpless, but this was a pain he had never witnessed. Not ever, in his entire career of discovering lies, deceit, greed, and crime, had he seen anyone more victimized or pained than Miss Evelyn Hughes. Yet the pain was not a victim's pain. It was an indescribable, tangible different kind of entity entirely.

Perhaps he should have expected for her to be strong, or intensely confident again. Maybe conceited, or selfish. Or even directing him on what to do at every turn. But this was raw and natural, and so, so very honest. To see her hair in such disarray, tangled in a way that he had failed to ever observe on any woman of his acquaintance, piqued his interest greatly.

Her freckles perfectly blended into the porcelain "English Rose" skin that so much of England's ladies strive for. Oh, the soot had streaked her face, but it was long gone as the tears washed it away.

He couldn't help but watch with awe as she cried as if he wasn't even watching. There was an intriguing strength to Evelyn Hughes that beckoned him and, if he was honest, beckoned him seductively.

And he was honest.

This pain was its own kind of beautiful; seeing her natural, softer, feminine side, was beguiling. She had affronted him in the past interactions, squared her shoulders, even put him in his place, but it wasn't who she was. He saw that now.

He loved this softer Miss Hughes, not with the proverbial heart, that is, but with an honorable respect and admiration. He felt the hairs on the back of his neck prickle, but his mind dismissed them.

Occupying the duke's land for months alone, except for her sister who was with child, and from the looks of it not far to go before her time was upon her, was a feat not to be scoffed at. What all had she sacrificed? What pain had she had to endure? Where were the men who should have protected her, and loved her?

This weeping woman had an intensely tender heart. The honest, raw ache radiating from her confirmed this to him.

Anyone who could feel pain this deeply, could also love this deeply.

He was kneeling at her feet, and she was still sitting on the log next to her sister. Without fully being aware of what he was doing he placed one hand on her right shoulder, then the other on her left. He did not know why he had done so and almost removed them, but he didn't.

He took a breath to calm himself. What was he doing? He could not embrace her, regardless of the strength of the impulse. Not with witnesses. He exhaled slowly, and carefully filled his chest again.

Remove your hands, Silence, he instructed himself.

Begging his mind to hunt for a reason why he was being so familiar with her, he failed, for his efforts were for naught.

Attempting to calm himself further he exhaled, but still he could not remove his hands from her shoulders. *This will not do!*

He held his breath momentarily at the end of the breath and slowly pulled it back in, hoping to come up with something to say before she came out of her trance. But his words failed him yet again. And Kenneth Silence was never silent.

He partook hungrily of another slow breath to gain control of himself.

He realized that her eyes were doing the conversing; in fact, communicating quite nicely to him. Interestingly, she was in no way resisting, which caused relief to fill his chest. He allowed himself to listen observantly to the nonverbal interaction. Moments became minutes and minutes were akin to hours, but knowing they were not.

The breaths came easier as he watched her gaze focus, her mouth close again, and her chest stop heaving. He smiled to himself. She really was beautiful, even as disheveled as she may have been described by anyone else.

But to Kenneth Silence she was stronger for showing such weakness, and that was magnificent.

His pleasant diversion was interrupted by her soft words of gratitude, "Thank you, that helped me to gain control."

Failing to hide his confusion, she further explained, "The breathing, it helped me. As you showed me how to slow my breath, I found what I needed to gather my senses. You calmed me so easily. I am at a loss to remember having anyone do that for me for quite some time. My mother used to calm me, though."

Hoping that the distraction would also be helpful, he asked, "Tell us about it as we walk to see the duke and duchess."

He removed his hands from her shoulders, stood, and offered a very strong arm to her. He was pleased that she took it readily, almost greedily. Or maybe it was he who took her arm hungrily. Either way, he was beyond pleased.

CHAPTER 12

Mr. and Mrs. Hughes were not always close; she knew that years waxed and waned in her own expression of affection, and sensed it was the same for her husband. She remembered the best year of their marriage was when Ester and Evelyn were eight, and he started taking them out about town without her. He was so very proud of them, which endeared her to him all the more.

Mr. Hughes had adored his daughters for approximately four or five more years, and then, with no apparent causation, he simply stopped escorting them around town. He hired people to come into their home, obsessively insisting that their friends called on them at Hughes House, and that his daughters must be supervised at all times. Mrs. Hughes did not think anything of it until Ester and Evelyn turned fourteen and needed to be more involved in society or, at the very minimum, go to the modiste to pick the fabric they wanted. But even that was asking too much. Her husband hovered, could even be considered overexcited, when he was not made aware of their whereabouts.

For many years, Mrs. Hughes never discovered the trigger for her husband's changed behavior towards Ester and Evelyn.

They were very different girls, though, and about this same time they blossomed and diverged from wanting to dress alike. Ester, the older by twelve minutes, tended towards enjoying one on one time but, strangely, enjoyed wearing brighter colors— contrasting with her conservative nature. And nearly the exact opposite was true with Evelyn, choosing blues and pale pinks and pale yellows.

The consistency of their natures stayed well into their coming out. Most of society knew Ester was the elder, but since she rarely went to the balls and Evelyn went to all of them, sometimes two in one night, society referred to the younger twin, Evelyn, as Miss Hughes.

This was where her thoughts were when her husband had come to her three days ago. It was not the first, and she knew it would not be the last.

"I will ask once more . . ."

"It is best you do not know where they are, dearest," she had said firmly.

"I am the head of the family; for once, let me decide what is best."

Mrs. Hughes bit her tongue. There was so much she wanted to say. Mr. Hughes' personality tended towards Ester, the reserved daughter, but that didn't change his opinions. His opinions were not so reserved. People simply perceived he had none, or at least assumed he was quite soft and flexible with his opinions.

"You know you make plenty of decisions. I am not in the position to do so for the estate or tenants."

Dipping his chin enough to fully gaze at her in disappointment, he marched off.

She exhaled. At least it had gone better this time.

*****

The marquess was becoming desperate. He asked the butler, "Where is Silence? Will he be returning shortly? I am obliged to wait. Or return when he is available."

"I cannot say, sir. He departed with few directions, and certainly not the direction to send his correspondence. I am expecting to hear from him soon, though. Would you like to leave your calling card, again?" He said the last word haughtily.

Mr. Grey, the Marquess of Tisdale, gave him a stern look. He had already left three. He then ran his hands smoothly over his slicked-back black hair, and exhaled. "You and I both know that is not necessary."

"Yes, sir." The butler moved to close the door to Silence's townhouse and Mr. Grey left the steps, inept at knowing what direction to head.

What had Silence been up to lately? Who hired him to be gone for over a week? Granted, he did not know Silence well, but knew he was the only one he could trust now. He just wished Kenneth Silence didn't know who Miss Hughes was already.

He couldn't risk asking any more people about her whereabouts.

But, somehow, he knew he could trust Silence.

*****

Evelyn was grateful for the strong arm of Mr. Silence to lean on. He wasn't shaking like she was. He seemed to have strength to push forward, but she just wished to sit down. She had never been this fatigued before, as if life drained from her marrow.

"Miss Hughes, tell me about your mother. You said she has helped you in the past."

She nodded, then channeled her focus away from each painful step. "Ironically, my mother can be exasperating, yet calming as well. One day she is calm and nurturing, another she is fidgety and distracted. But on the days she is the former, I cannot get enough of her. She sees me."

"She sees you? But she does not admit you into her presence the other days?"

"Of course she does, everyday, but maybe it is better said that she feels me, or sees me in her life. On those days she is in tune with my needs and desires. It isn't every day, for being married to my father is not easy, but she tries harder than any lady I know."

"Tries to do what?"

"I do not rightly know." Evelyn let out a single laugh. She had never tried to qualify it before. "But she tries. As if trying will make things go more smoothly, or if she tries to better herself, or to be there for my needs, or to learn a new skill, that . . . I am not sure how to finish that sentence. At times I feel she is racing against someone, but I worry that someone is herself. If she slows down and is still, the self she is running from catches up and she becomes distracted, locked down in her mind, and that is when she stops seeing me. I cannot describe how painful it is to watch her writhe away from herself all over again. But once she pushes ahead, gains the upper hand on whatever she is running from, she breathes again. Then she has the time, or the calmness of mind to attend to me."

"How does she attend to you?"

They had arrived at the staircase that led down into the ravine, and she saw that there were tools, a new piece of wood, bailing wire, and a dimming lantern. "Were you— were you fixing the top stair in the dark?" She looked at him incredulously.

"No." His face flushed red and he put his hand to his head. "Yes, there was no daylight, but I had a lantern."

She just stared at him.

"I am not all that docked in the head. Truly. I often enjoy an early morning ride . . . and I accepted, or rather demanded to see you at tea . . . and I had plans already to assist Gavin in the afternoon. So I rightly did not imagine this stair being fixed until evening anyway except, when I returned last night, Grace begged me to ask you to come to dinner tonight. And I could not allow you to descend the stairs one more time without it being properly secured. By my calculation, it meant it had to be fixed before my early morning ride."

"So that is why you were here? At the wee hours of the morning?"

"Forgive me?" he requested with a small smile.

"Of course, I cannot imagine how things would have turned out if you had not." Her mind went dark momentarily, and then she realized she finally had her thing to be grateful for. Two things. Silence was there then, as well as here now.

"Well, good intentions have left us without a top step. As you can see, I have already removed the old one. Allow me to release your arm while I finish the step. It should not take long."

She nodded and removed her arm, stepping a small distance to the right, and kneeled down in the grass. This left the rock for her sister; Eddie acknowledged this, and led her sister to sit as well.

Silence immediately knelt down and said, "Well, one good thing is there is sun now to light the project." He put out the lantern and set it to the side. Without looking up, he probed, "Tell me more about your mother. How is it she attends you."

"In motherly ways, I suppose. My favorite is when she mindlessly plays with my hair, or applies cream to my hands, rubbing them for over an hour in the most delightful way. Both have put me to sleep before. It relaxes me so much, especially when she does the hair. When I was younger I would intentionally exaggerate my fatigue in church, and she would guide my head to her lap and I would enjoy an hour of her combing it with her fingers, or rubbing my ear. When I would peek up at her she wasn't even watching me, but mindlessly doing it, naturally, while she listened to the sermon."

By now he was on his stomach, leaning over the ledge with the bailing wire. He looked towards her briefly and asked, "How often would you do this?"

"Every Sunday."

Her sister spoke up, "Not every Sunday, for I gained some sense and learned to be fatigued first."

They both smiled, and Evelyn lay her head on the knee of her older twin sister.

*****

While making quick work of securing the new stair, Kenneth watched from the corner of his eye as the two sisters took turns conversing, smiling, and also enjoying each other in nonverbal ways that only two very close sisters could do. He wondered which one was older. But as Ester mindlessly twirled Evelyn's hair, in a very protective, motherly fashion, he was pretty sure he knew. Which would also explain why so many of the reports in town of "The Eldest Miss Hughes" being taciturn, submissive, and not liking to go out in society, did not describe Evelyn Hughes in anyway.

Even after a tragedy like the fire they were grooming each other, soothing each other in a very tender, yet unconscious way. One sister would move, and the other would accommodate. It was like they were a left hand and a right hand, working together equally, but differently.

They did not look like each other but appeared to be the same age, so he was going to deduce that they were twins, mostly by the way they had identical mannerisms.

How had he failed to understand there were two Miss Hugheses? He was so intrigued with this absence of truth, but now the persistent headache he experienced in the recent past now made sense. The men at the club were telling the truth, but it was inconsistent with what he knew was also the truth.

He accidently chuckled when he figured that out.

Evelyn noticed his single laugh, and she asked, "Is everything well?"

"Yes, thank you. The step is just about done. So, are you twins?"

They both giggled and nodded.

"I was not aware your sister was at the cottage with you." Speaking to Ester, he said, "You hid yourself well. Perhaps a bit more of your sister's secrecy and reservation can be better explained with this new bit of information."

His inviting comment hung in the air, for more time than he expected, before they replied.

Ester rubbed her abdomen and said, "For good reason. My husband is not—"

"—not here," Evelyn finished, with even greater reservation than usual.

Kenneth's hair stood up on the back of his neck, and the subtlest twinge of pain started in his head. It was the first time that Evelyn had evoked his gift, albeit in a very minor way.

The two looked at each other, and a silent battle ensued. Ester, however, was the one who spoke first. "I have heard you offer assistance in various ways to those who might need help. What exactly do you do?"

"Ester . . ."

"Come now, Evie, we need help. I want to go home." She motioned with her head to the smoking cottage, and said, "There is no denying it. We need help. Not just me, but you do, too. I have watched you take every burden on, but we must reach to those who, clearly," and she motioned to Silence, "want to help. Mr. Silence, what are you known for?"

"Silence."

"I seriously doubt that. Do you mean you are good at keeping confidences?" Ester asked.

He chuckled, "No. Well, yes, I am. However, I was just correcting you on my name. Just call me Silence." He cleared his throat and returned to her question. "I am an investigator, a hired secret-finder. I learn what others cannot, and in return I have food on my plate and clothes on my back. Sometimes it is the local gentry who need to know who is stealing from them, or where or how their father died, or other times it is the English parliament that needs my help."

"Ye're a spy?" Eddie asked in a heavy brogue, then mumbled something in Irish that sounded like a swear word he had heard in a pub a few times.

"What? No. I certainly do not dabble in politics or take sides, except being loyal to my own moral platform. I mean to say I am hired to learn who plans to vote one way or another, and then others will be able to focus their attention on swaying them."

Evelyn quickly added, "So you *share* secrets for a living." Then she looked knowingly at her sister, as if the silent conversation from earlier had been decided, with herself as the victor.

The step was now secure; it wasn't going anywhere for a good ten years. So he stood, dusted himself off, and walked over to the sisters.

"I discover secrets or, more accurately, lies, that have been hurting people, suppressing their own or other's happiness. I do not do anything more than find out falsehoods and bring them to light. Miss Ester, Miss Evelyn, you clearly fall into this category of being suppressed, with no advocate but a single servant. You do not even have to pay me. Let me help you."

Ester quickly replied, "Of course we will pay you; that is, our father will."

Evelyn sucked in a breath.

The sisters continued the nonverbal battle momentarily, and finally, after a prolonged moment, Evelyn sighed, "Yes, of course we will hire you, Silence. We most definitely could use an advocate."

CHAPTER 13

There was no question that the ladies should be escorted to a guest room to rest after such a traumatic event. The Duke and Duchess of Huntington made sure to direct a servant to prepare biscuits and the latest heated chocolate drink immediately.

All the while no one asked, and no one spoke either, of the elephant in the room. Or the elephants, to be more precise, as there were a hundred questions that they all seemed to be eloquently dancing around. To Silence, the stench of the absence of answers was truly foul.

He played their game, though, and hung his head even when he would rather look them in the eye.

Grace was kind, solicitous, but did not ask why the ladies both shown up at the wee hours of the morning, with neither cloak nor proper gown. Perhaps it was that Eddie was with them, with his cheek abrasion that was unmistakably fresh, all the while dabbing at the back of his head where someone had struck him from behind.

One thing Silence *did* know was his own irritation was swelling far faster than the bruised, bleeding cheekbone on the manservant's face.

He took a deep breath to chill his temper, momentarily catching the attention of all in the room. Grace froze. Gavin glanced briefly to him, and of course looked away. And then they would suck in a breath, or even exhale, like it would push the tension from the room.

So Kenneth stayed silent. No one was going to explain anything this morning. That message was the only clear thought in his head.

When they had first squeezed through the small tunnel opening in the sitting room, Ester's protuberant abdomen barely fitting, the sisters had been wrapped in throws. Their hair was pushed aside and faces assessed thoroughly. The group of them had a language that was intense, but oh, so silent. Fear, concern, confusion, and anxiety were the predominant nonverbal sentences, however, in putting them all together. The final unspoken message was that Silence was the outsider.

He was not to know, at least not yet.

I always know! No matter what!

The soot alone should have prompted hundreds of questions from Gavin and Grace. The incredible lack of appropriate attire of the ladies should have been the start of the interrogation of the decade. Neither was there a cascade of concern for their safety, or why they were there.

It was almost as if they all knew what happened.

But Kenneth Silence did not know.

*****

Silence was willing, even able, to stay silent—but he had never been good at it. While the ladies were attended to with warm baths, better beds than they had had in months, and likely better-prepared food, Silence was lurking.

Oh yes, do not doubt that Kenneth Silence knew how to lurk, but it was likely coming off broody, like his good friend, Fitzwilliam Darcy of Pemberley. Now, *that* man was quite the exemplar to emulate.

He waited in the sitting room, an elbow on the mantel and recited the kings of the last century in order. Noticing that his fists were clenched, he commanded himself to portray no more concern than any of the others in the room.

Grace was painstakingly working on needlepoint. In and out. Slow and steady. You could hear the purr of the thread as it was pulled through the screen.

All it did was encourage Silence in this battle.

If they would not talk about what happened, he would not either.

The chimes of the eleventh hour almost derailed him. Almost. However, remembering the queens of the last century proved a harder challenge than he proposed.

There was a moment where he could not remember who ruled the throne for the few years before the Stuarts. He knew that it was the son of Oliver Cromwell, and that it was either Robert or Richard. However, the wife was the name that baffled him. It was such a good distraction, this naming game he had devised, that he forgot the unspoken rule of silence and asked, "I cannot make out something— might you assist me?"

Both Gavin and Grace looked up sheepishly, nodding like puppets.

"Was it Richard or Robert Cromwell? The one who was a terrible lead for the commonwealth? And who the dickens was his wife?"

Grace smiled slowly, while at the same time furrowing her brow. "I believe it was Dorothy Maihor who was Richard Cromwell's wife."

They all chuckled lightly at the absurdity of the questions, breaking the silence and tension that had been there before. To have held off discussing the fire, at the expense of all conversation, was like throwing the baby out with the bath water. And Silence even said that very thing to them.

"You are correct," Gavin said, "I should have tried to explain that, without the Hughes sisters' permission, we cannot discuss what happened, their circumstances, or anything related to what occupies all of our thoughts. But we can certainly converse about the monarchs of the last two centuries." Which, of course, prompted more laughter.

After that, the conversation crept in naturally.

*****

Finally, around late afternoon, Silence left the duke and duchess to their private ruminations and secrets, and went to his chambers. The day turned out not to be as full as he had expected, and longer than the Great Wall of China, too.

The Hughes sisters did not stir or come out of their chambers all day. From what he could tell, the duke didn't give any direct commands either. What was wrong with these people? Shouldn't they be investigating the fire? Or seeing if there was anything to salvage?

As antsy as he was, he trusted the Duke of Huntsman, and he had no doubt that Miss Evelyn Hughes was a highly intelligent woman who gave great thought to what she did, or didn't do. And Grace, the duchess, had more heart than anyone he knew, and would mother a frog or wild rabbit if it looked to be in need.

He paced in his room briefly, and looked to the west. Of course, this late in the day the smoke had cleared. There was no evidence from this far away, and there was no way to see the cottage remains, either, from Fleetwood Place.

Immediately, he knew he could not resist any longer; he'd made up his mind. He had never investigated a fire, but he knew enough to know it was likely arson. However, speculation was ill mannered in his line of work. He wanted proof. Evidence.

In early July no one would have had a fire going at night, which was the most common cause of house fires. Besides, he hadn't been able to suppress his need to check the premises of the cottage prior to working on the damaged stairs.

Nor had there been any rain, and therefore no lightning— the second-most-likely cause of fire.

It was night, and the fire seemed to start quickly, for there was no warning in any way until it was completely out of control.

There was no way this could have been an accident.

He had already changed long ago into clean clothes, but now he knew it was time to get dirty again.

*****

Evelyn was hungry. But she did not particularly want to see everyone, nor rehearse things over in her head any longer either. She just wished she could be sure of the way to the servants' staircase down to the kitchen from this room. It wasn't far; when she and Ester first came from London back in December, they had spent a fortnight on this floor while the cottage was being made hospitable. She made up her mind to try every door if necessary at the end of the hall.

She slowly opened the door, pleased it made no sound, but not so pleased to see that Eddie was asleep in a chair just outside her door.

Evelyn started to tiptoe around Eddie, his odiferous hat covering his face. As she stepped, the floor squeaked. She paused, hoping to push through his slumber. The man was offered a bed, but he insisted on camping in the hall at the entrance to the sisters' chambers, to keep watch. Remembering the argument was enough to make her want to laugh. Never before had she heard such Irish profanities slicing the air. He gave stubborn a new name.

After a brief pause, she tried to proceed past her one-man guard. His breathing hitched slightly but then continued under the hat, slow and steady again. Once she was past him by at least two paces, she placed her foot on an aggravatingly loud floorboard. Grimacing, she halted, turned back to see if it had woken him. There Eddie was, hovering over her, assessing her disapprovingly.

The hunter had caught his game, and she put her hands on her hips.

In the heaviest brogue yet, Eddie said, "Miss Evelyn, you are always in the field when luck is on the road."

She raised one finger to her friend's face and said, "Surprisingly, I understand the deeply Irish-accented words, but the meaning escapes me. And this time, I demand you tell me what that meant."

"Aye, ye shall be told. Without dishonoring you, you never cease to get into trouble, and when a good thing is upon ye, ye bury yer head in the dirt."

Evelyn tried to filter the second metaphor. To what was he referring? She said as much to him, too, when any other retort did not readily come.

"Why turn away from the one who can help? Luck is upon you; do not turn back to the plow."

"Good Lord, Eddie, stop speaking in metaphors. What do you mean?"

"Ye need help. You accepted help just this morning, so there should be not a hair displaced from your head from this day onward from your own sweat and effort. Besides, it is not just Ester who needs the protectin', and ye knows it. Now, about face and return to yer chambers. I'll order ye some hot water. No more work for either one of you. You are a guest in the duke's home. Not on his lands, mind you, 'cause you are here safe. Now that you are up, I best be headin' off with the man who has been watching you noisily creep out your chambers as if no one could hear you."

She glanced down the hall, where Eddie had gestured, and where Silence was smirking, fully dressed in his riding coat and pants. Had he really watched her tiptoe down the hall, attempting to evade her ever-loyal servant?

Silence took a few graceful strides to her and stopped in front of her, pausing to bow briefly. The smirk was replaced with concern and he asked, "What is it you needed? How can I be of service?"

"I, ah, to be honest, I wanted a biscuit or two and cold milk. Oh, the thought of cold milk sounds so tempting; I have not had that delicacy for ages."

He offered his arm and said, "Come. How do lemon fennel biscuits sound? The cook made a fresh batch while you slept. I have already had my share, as well as the ones that Eddie should have eaten, but he insisted on standing guard until you woke. He would not eat a bite of anything until you two did."

Evelyn looked behind her and smiled to Eddie in gratitude. He tipped his shapeless hat in her direction then returned to his position in the chair, watching over her sister. "Then let us ensure he has some sent to him."

"So we shall."

Evelyn sensed Kenneth wanted to say more, so she returned her gaze to her escort. "Yes?"

"It can wait." They started walking down the hall.

His gentle arm she was holding on to was strong and defined, yet somehow she felt a gentleness, or cautiousness in his touch.

She knew it was time to help him understand. He would have to be told if he was going to be of any help.

"No; no, it cannot. I know you wish for answers. Let me start by saying that Ester is married to a sailor, and was married before . . . well . . ." She seemed to choke on the words.

"Yes, yes, before . . ." He seemed to have just as hard a time as she was in mentioning that her sister was with child.

Had she ever, ever in her entire life, spoken of this topic with a man? Never.

She cleared her throat and continued. Silence apparently knew the way.

"It was still a scandal. Ester eloped with him when our father refused his blessing. That is what happened the night of the Halliburtons' party. We came home to find her note, and by then she was hours ahead of us. The weather did not allow for riding after her, but he sent servants anyway."

"If I remember correctly the night started clear, but I ruined a jacket walking home in the rain."

"You have a sharp memory." She let out a sigh and continued. "He told us he had lost quite a bit at the gaming tables, and had asked all of us to leave the party early. I am sure you must have thought it was your sparks and tricks at the pianoforte that was the cause of my hastened departure, but that is not the case. My father had met his match at the tables that night. That is a feat, of course, as my father is a wizard at cards. He tried to teach me once, how you could count them, and use predictions of winning hands. But I never desired to play cards. My father rarely loses, and when he does it matters little because he is always temperate in his bets. But he was quite flustered that night. I am not aware of the particulars, but I know I had never seen him that way. I am assuming the stakes were high, and so early in the evening, too. He kept saying, 'Not again. Not again.'"

Kenneth simply listened as she continued. "The next month would be our twenty-first birthday. We would be of age. Ester eloped to Gretna Green, just before the time she could have been allowed to marry, if they had just had the banns read. We all knew that father did not want her marring a third son. She understood this, but has not provided a reasonable answer for eloping."

"Yes, once of age she would no longer need her father's blessing." His voice was smooth, and encouraging.

But she was not in need of encouragement. She wanted to talk about it. She wanted his help. "We have learned since then that my father, years ago, lost a major card game. Lives were at stake. Do you catch my meaning? Our father bet my sister's hand in marriage to someone, an unknown man to us, when we were twelve. Ester was by far prettier than me then and, of course, the elder."

As they entered the kitchen, he said, "You both are very handsome. Although, the hideous bonnets must go."

Shocked that he would tease her so at a time like this, she nonetheless smiled at him. She whispered, "Thank you." She let out her guarded breath. He would probably assume she was saying thank you for the compliment. But she was not.

She judged him wrong, for he knew she did not express gratitude for the kindness.

"For what?" he asked.

"For not judging my father. He feels miserable over it. And has suffered with the weight of what he did for years. He is an honorable man, though. He would have kept his word. She would have been forced to wed."

They found the pot of biscuits and began nibbling on them. Mr. Silence seemed to probe a bit, "But your sister, she discovered it." It was said as a statement, not a question, and that confused her.

"Oh no, she did not. It was coincidence that she eloped," she said.

"I do not believe in coincidences. I believe in motive."

Evelyn furrowed her brow a bit while simultaneously chewing the biscuit. She tilted her head and questioned, "I do not think I fully catch your meaning. At least I hope not."

"I am saying that maybe Ester knows more than she has told you."

Quickly shaking her head, she defiantly said, "Oh no, that is not the case. You are not a twin. Secrets can be detected between us."

For some reason he scoffed briefly.

But she persisted. "I can sense when my sister is withholding something, no matter how big or small it is. There is no way she knew she was going to be forced to marry a stranger."

For the first time ever, Evelyn wondered if it was possible for Ester to have kept a secret from her. And as she looked into the sympathetic hazel eyes of Kenneth Silence, she knew that it was possible.

Because Evelyn had been keeping from her sister just how much she was falling in love with Kenneth Silence.

CHAPTER 14

Kenneth watched Miss Hughes eat her biscuits, savoring them as if they were of the finest quality. He did not want to press her for more information, but it still didn't explain why they had to leave society, and especially didn't explain why someone set fire to the cottage. Everything she had said was true, even the part that her father had felt miserable about betting the marriage of his eldest child. That is, until she said that Ester did not know about the bet. He couldn't be sure about that. He understood that Evelyn Hughes felt it was true, but anyone with common sense would have doubted it, too.

She had babbled a bit while eating, without getting to the answers he sought. Evelyn had said that she had to do chores because, like her father had said in the emancipation papers, as he liked to call them, "Learning who you want to be is far more precious a lesson than who people tell you to be."

But the riddle of all riddles came when she quoted more from the emancipation letter that sent her to the cottage on the duke's land, "Live for love and therefore love to live, or to live for other's love." It just did not sound like a father's words. A mother's, maybe.

One of the scullery maids rushed into the room, but started backing out while apologizing when she noticed them.

Silence reached in her direction. "No, wait. Miss, might you have some fresh milk for the lady?"

"Yes, sir." She dipped a little awkwardly and hurried from the room, but was not gone long.

Once the scullery maid delivered the milk and retreated from the room again, he turned back to Evelyn, who sat across from where he was standing. She had freshened up a bit but had failed to do anything but a simple braid with her beautiful red hair. It was loosely braided, with the twisting beginning past her shoulders. He had the opportunity to see that when she was tiptoeing from her room past Eddie. But now, from his perspective, it almost appeared her hair was down again, like when he saw her on the swing.

The memory alone of her hair flowing and gown blowing in the wind was enough to make Silence readjust his standing position, and he took a seat. He felt the room was a bit warm, too. He refocused his mind on the task at hand.

"Forgive me, Miss Evelyn, but you will need to share all you know. If your sister—forgive me, what is your sister's married name?"

She smiled widely. "Oh, how lovely it is to speak it aloud to someone other than my sister. Thomas. Mrs. Ester Thomas." Her pride in her statement was endearing.

"If Mrs. Thomas was married before she was," he cleared his throat, "with child, why run away? And where is Mr. Thomas?"

"He is earning a living or, more precisely, securing one. He is a third son. Initially, when they returned, my father was furious. Pacing night and day. That is when he shared with us that she was promised to another. For two weeks he was threatening annulment, and we were both confined to the house. Phillip was only admitted with a chaperone, but I am afraid I was a terrible choice, for I was a, ah, shall we say, sympathetic chaperone." She looked down at her hands and started examining them.

There was an element of guilt as she said these next words. "I believe this is the main reason he did not give us any servants besides Eddie. My father's letter wanted us to 'learn what it meant to be a lady of society. You should crave what you were born with.'"

It was hard to explain why he felt some unkind feelings toward their father. He seemed to rule by the law, and not the heart.

Nevertheless, he understood her meaning, which meant annulment was off the table. Which also explained how she became with child so soon.

He waited patiently for the rest of what she knew.

"Perhaps I was sympathetic a few times. My mother suspected it as well, and one morning while my father was out, she read me a letter he had written. It was directing Phillip and Ester to go to Gavin and Grace's estate temporarily, where further instructions would be given. I, of course, chose to go with them. But within a fortnight my mother stated the man was searching for Ester, and the unfortunate thing was he was demanding that if Ester could not be found, then he would demand alternative and equal settlement of the debt . . ."

"You. He was requiring to marry you if Ester was not provided."

She nodded and looked down at her hands on the table.

"Yes, this man, whoever it was, knew we would be turning of age shortly, and supposedly was making threats to our father. That is why they sent us so urgently in the middle of the night. My mother told me that, although furious, Father really wished to say goodbye. However, negotiating with the man at his residence was the best way to ensure that the man never knew we left."

Silence pondered this bit of information. He had a tingle of suspicion that told him that last sentence did not add up.

What was it? What part was incorrect? Was the father more involved? It was hard to imagine a father sending them away without so much as a goodbye. Or warning. Silence shook his head a bit. No decent father would, at least. He was beginning to suspect there were parts of the story of which she was unaware.

Evelyn continued, "We had little time to pack anything more than a trunk each. Most of Ester's clothes have had to be altered, but Father sent more money as the months went on or the need was even hinted at. If I asked, I found it was given. For the most part."

Under his breath, Silence smirked while saying, "I see you are very sympathetic chaperone, but not sympathetic enough to voice your needs. You are a gentleman's daughter; you should not have been doing manual labor."

Her only reply, for he knew she heard him, was a heavy sigh.

It was not what he expected. A good portion of him had been honest in his statement, but the better portion of him wanted to spar again.

The conversation had been heavy. And they had only begun.

Glancing her way to assess why she had not taken the bait, he saw a kindness and contentment in her gaze. She was not at all affronted. And there was plenty of gratitude in her dreamy enjoyment of her biscuit, but there was a whole lot more enjoyment on his part as he savored her beauty.

He wondered how she was blessed with a uniquely beautiful color of strawberry, blonde, and auburn hair color. There were highlights at the common areas framing the face that brought in bits of blonde, but the tricolored array was not one he had ever seen—noticed, yes—for that was something that was difficult not to notice each time they met. That, and her extremely small waist.

How many times had he imagined placing his hands at the tempting outward curve that descended from that small waist? Maybe even allowing the liberty of using the hips to pull her to him for a kiss. He could not lie, it was more than a few. As a matter of fact, it was the predawn imaginations that very morning that convinced him to fix the step so early like he had. One thing a bachelor learns quickly is that physical labor has its benefits. Today, splitting wood would not have been more useful than actually rescuing the ladies of the cottage.

He had dwelled on his ruminations too long, so he prodded with his other questions. "Where is Mr. Thomas now? At sea?"

"I assume so. The last letter that he sent indicated that he was an understudy for the captain of a small company that owns a cargo fleet. I believe the last letter we sent three weeks ago has not been answered. That is, unless Ester has kept it to herself."

"Are these the letters she sacrificed herself to save from the fire?"

"One and the same. They write almost weekly; in fact, it actually is weekly because I drop the letter off every week when I have tea with the duchess."

"I think you need to ask her to hand over the letters. I would like to read them."

Silence was surprised when she outright laughed at him.

"Oh, I would sorely like to see you make that suggestion to my sister! She will not even let *me* read them!"

He raised an eyebrow, betting Evelyn would understand how serious a game they were in.

She repeated the gesture and added a raised, firm jaw. She had met his bet, even raising the stakes.

He turned his head to the side and honored hers, raising his jaw as well in defiance.

The battle had begun months before. Bets were now finally being called in.

He added to his confident deck of cards a heaviness of brow, darkening the moment. At least he hoped he did. In truth, it was the best bluffing game he had played yet.

She bit her lip in mock fretfulness. Or was it? Could he be losing this silent tête-à-tête?

The lip did look so delicious against her teeth.

Stay the course.

He couldn't. He grinned.

She proudly smiled in delight.

Had he somehow folded? "Will you at least ask her for me?"

"Oh no, that little game was to have you let me watch *you* ask her for them. I am delighted at the result. What a clear capture of my favorite opponent."

He wiggled his eyebrow flirtatiously and doubled down with her one more time in his most enticing baritone, "Favorite?"

Her smile quickly slipped away and she swallowed hard, color rising brightly to her cheeks. "Perhaps favorite is too strong a word. Perhaps 'least distasteful'."

He bellowed his delight and gladly folded. "Very well, you shall be present."

He was beginning to realize that having her present, anytime, would be a delight. What a gift that would be.

*****

She already missed him. She had excused herself from the servants' area after calling him her "favorite opponent". She had not lost a battle of wits in ages. And certainly not by showing her true feelings! *I called him my favorite opponent!*

The very word brought up goose flesh on her arms again. She prayed he hadn't noticed then, and prayed that the maid only assumed it was from tepid bathwater now. She had basked in the once-hot water for what felt like an hour, most of which doing nothing other than thinking about Silence.

She tried to shift thoughts towards finding out how the fire was started. Suddenly she had the thought that made her jump from the water and ask the maid to help her dress.

Time was of the essence, or at least to her untrained mind it was.

Once she was dressed the maid insisted on plaiting her hair, which she swore would take no more than a few minutes more, and she lived up to that easily.

She raced down the stairs, searching the rooms until she found them, and breathlessly said, "Honey . . . Honeymae did not bark."

She scanned the room and saw the duke sit up straighter. Eddie slowly nodded in awareness and Grace looked rather confused.

All eyes, especially Silence's, were on her to explain. "Honeymae did not alert us, which means she knew the person who started the fire. Someone close to us started the fire to hurt us. She would have barked at a stranger."

She looked to Silence first, as if it was the missing piece; the only piece needed. How naïve she was.

Silence stated dryly, "It was definitely arson; I just returned from investigating the site. But this new information narrows down the suspects significantly. How many do you think would be on the list? Do not hold back out of fear or denial that they could or would do it. Finding the arsonist is my job; yours is to be forthcoming with any information available."

She nodded before adding, "Only a few besides family."

"Let us start there—"

"Pardon me? You have sorely forgotten yourself. No one in my family would have—"

His persona changed, and suddenly she felt like she was in the presence of the constable. "The list, madam. Do not forget that your mother and father are some of the few people who know where you lived."

Now there were only a few who knew Evelyn well enough to know she was extremely protective of her family. Look what she had done for Ester! She had spent months protecting her!

The fury started to build, but then she saw Silence gaze at her with understanding. "Miss Hughes, I do know that this is difficult for you. But unless we have an excellent understanding of where the danger is, you and your sister will always be in hiding."

He stepped a little closer and continued, "I would never accuse anyone until there was no longer any measurable doubt that he or she had done it. In other words there must be proof, and you have hired me to find the proof. I ask for your assistance—no, I require it."

He or she? It had not occurred to her that it could possibly be a woman! She hadn't thought hard enough. She took a breath, attempting to be more compliant to the methods that seemed foreign to her. "Most of my previous household handled Honeymae; that is the butler, three housemaids, three footman, my father's valet, and at least one gardener, just to name a few. The cook could not stand her, nor my mother's lady's maid. She was just beginning to warm up to my father's steward, but still did not like him much."

Eddie cleared his throat. "How many of them lady's maids are as tall as me?"

She quirked her head to the side. "None; there are few men who are as tall as you."

"Thank you kindly."

Silence had a curious look on his face and he opened his mouth to ask, but Eddie supplied the answer.

"Whoever hit me on the head was mighty tall. They hit me first on the back of me head, but it didn't knock me out. Not like how ye found me. Oh, I stumbled a little, buzzed, like me bell was wrung good, but then when they saw I didn't go down they wrapped their arms around my throat from behind. They squeezed me, and if I hadn't been so buzzed I could 'ave taken 'im. But I was so off kilter, that up was to the right and down was to the left, and what should have been straight lines was curved. Never felt so discombobulated. But not too many can keep their arms around me throat from behind without losing their footing as I whirled every which way. And he smelled, too; something awful."

Silence pitched in and asked, "What did he smell like?"

"Like when the cook hangs all the herbs from the garden in the shed to dry. Combined with the smell of salt pork that is curing. Earthy. Sour, and dry. I do not know how else to explain it." Eddie huffed under his breath in his heavy brogue, "I'm as fit to mind mice in a crossroads." He stood up and started pacing. "I should be more helpful, but I ain't no scholar, nor a cook. I suppose it would be more accurate to say it was some kind of herb, or spice."

Evelyn gasped.

"What is it?" Grace asked.

"The marquess smells like cloves. It is quite noticeable, too." She thought to herself, *and he is very tall*. She hadn't needed to say the last part anyway; she saw Silence's awareness as he fit the puzzle pieces together

"Eddie, could it be cloves?" Evelyn bravely asked.

"Aye, I'd say that is it exactly. Cloves, ehh, not a smell I prefer."

It was not possible to hold back the shiver.

CHAPTER 15

They had been hiding in London for two weeks now. Not even Mr. and Mrs. Hughes knew their daughters had all been transplanted to Silence's townhouse.

Grace and Gavin had returned to their townhouse as well, to be of assistance.

The hardest part was that Honeymae had to be left at the duke's house. The giant dog was so noticeable, even recognizable, and her bark couldn't be muffled. There had been no rebuttal to the suggestion. Her dearest companion was being cared for by Eddie, even though she was likely the key to it all. The plan was to wait until the last possible moment, when Silence had all his facts prepared.

Ester was feeling quite uncomfortable the last several days, even being willing to complain, which was a rarity. They had sent a letter to her husband, letting him know that she was safe, and now in London. She had included that Silence's household was equipped with a well-experienced matriarch of the kitchen who could handle the laying-in when her time was upon her.

There were no parties to attend, no rides in Hyde Park, no invitations to even decline.

She sighed, and reviewed what Silence had discovered so far.

Mr. Grey had courted her for several weeks, even before tragedy took his uncle, leaving him as the next Marquess of Tisdale. Mr. Harrison Grey had apparently been calling on Silence daily while he was at the duke's. He had needed Silence's covert help.

Help finding Evelyn.

The chills started again.

But then she remembered Silence's comforting words when he told her the plan to take the job the marquess was hiring Silence for: *"I agreed to find you for him; I did not agree to deliver you into his hands. Whether you trust me or not, I know I can keep you safe. This way I can find out directly from him what he knows, and his purpose in finding you."*

She was going to be safe.

*****

Silence paced. Another week went by and still no true direction to go. It was irritating him beyond belief. Oh, the leads were plenty, but none of them had any traction. He stopped pacing again and pretended to read his book in the garden, but truly it was simply a chance for him to rehearse all the conversations with the marquess. At least the important parts.

It was late July and the ladies had only been safely hidden for twenty-four hours when he returned the call to the marquess.

"I do hope you are well," Silence had said when he was admitted to the marquess' library. He took off his hat and placed it on the side table.

"Silence, I have no time for kindnesses. I need your investigatory skills. Time is of the essence. I must find Miss Hughes, as she is in danger. Do you remember her from the Halliburtons' party?"

Silence helped himself to the brandy. What he said was true. She was in danger, and he did want to find her. "The Miss Evelyn Hughes I remember from the dinner party is not one I wish to remember."

"Still sore, are you? I did not take you for a sensitive chap. Well, we are more alike than you think."

Silence just wanted to assist the marquess in disclosing all, and keep his headache to a minimum. He handed the single glass of brandy to the marquess and he took it willingly.

"Why is she in danger?"

After a hefty gulp he blurted out, "I want to marry her." He choked a bit and added, "Me marrying her is not why she is in danger. It is why I want to find her."

Silence would have laughed at the irony if he had not been so worried that this man was an arsonist and had attacked Eddie. Instead he just continued to ask more direct questions.

"Who is after her?"

"I cannot say."

He took a heavy breath and exhaled slowly, waiting for him to explain.

"It is not him I am protecting, you see. It is Miss Hughes."

So it was a man, not a woman, which was already presumed with knowing that it was a tall attacker. And the first part was the clearest lie he had heard in some time. He was protecting someone, and it could very well be himself. But the way he had said it, as if there really was another person, made him begin to doubt that the Marquess of Tisdale, or Mr. Grey, was who they were looking for.

"Just to be clear, which Miss Hughes are we talking about? From what I understand, the society papers state the twin sisters have not been seen in months."

"Eight months, to be exact. And to answer your question, both."

"Tell me what I need to know."

The marquess paused, took out his pocket watch, and cringed. "Come back tomorrow morning and we will ride. I do not even trust my help to know this information."

"Do you have somewhere to be?"

"What? Oh, no."

Silence watched the marquess purse his lips, which was usually a sign of dishonesty. Unfortunately he needed no sign, and his head reminded him of that.

When Silence still hadn't said anything Grey continued, his speech somewhat pressured. "I was replying to several dinner invitations, a boring task for sure, but I imbibed far too much before you called. And as you can see, I have finished what you gave me. I'd like a clear head. The Halliburtons are having an Autumn Masquerade. Will you be going?"

He had changed the subject.

Silence just smiled and waited.

"Please, Silence, tell me you will help me find her, and find her soon. Why are you being so quiet?"

He nodded in acknowledgement that it was different than his usual character. "My work-self is often less dandy-like. I will be happy to find the Misses Hughes."

As he was shown out, Kenneth knew two things. One, he was going to the Halliburtons' masquerade, and two, he was going to have to tail the marquess tonight instead of being in the presence of his new houseguests.

And he confirmed one other thing. The smell of cloves was strong, and a bit pungent.

Silence tapped the top of his top hat and descended the marquess' front steps, whispering to himself, "Lead on, Mr. Grey."

Remembering the first interaction led right into what happened next.

It was not late enough in the day to be conspicuous in following him, but Silence kept his distance anyway. He had enough experience with tracking someone that he knew how to keep his head low, but to always know what surrounds you. Twice Grey looked behind him, but more often he was looking down the side streets.

Left, right, his neck was straining. He was looking for someone. He didn't seem worried that anyone would be following him, but it was he who was tracking someone else.

The sudden halt of Silence's target, six meters ahead, made Silence hunker down behind the two ladies with a parasol. They smiled at him, and he nodded, just in time to see that Grey had hurried down the right alleyway.

Kenneth was able to shuffle off the flirtations with apologies for following the ladies so closely, just in time to see the marquess pass a note to a small boy, not more than six or seven years old. The street urchin had been reselling older newspapers, because when the coins from Grey were dropped in one hand the old newspapers in the other hand made friends with the cobblestone alley.

The boy ran further down the alley, and Kenneth retreated from his location just as Grey about-faced to return to Piccadilly Square.

Kenneth had two options. He chose to stay on the marquess' tail.

Looking back, he wondered if he should have followed the poor child. He hadn't even had a good look at him. But he took note of the alley he was located in.

Kenneth Silence was not a man who enjoyed cigar smoke, and being forced to endure it was frustrating. There was a man loitering just around the corner.

He had assumed that since the marquess did not trust his staff, only he could directly deliver a note to a boy who would deliver a note to another person for a few coins. Either there would be a visitor to the marquess, or the marquess had a meeting set up. The evening had turned to night very quickly after the interaction with the young boy, and Silence was beginning to doubt that there was anything to wait for.

But no one came, and Grey never left.

But one cigar-smoking man stayed the same length of time that Silence did.

He did not think the man was a threat, because he was doing nothing but smoking a cigar and primping. A tug here or there on a suit coat, a dusting of the arms and, of course, the smoothing of the slicked-back hair. At times Silence thought he looked familiar. But the heat from the day probably got to him.

Finally, Kenneth Silence went home. But the investigator in him chose to take the long way home, right past the man with the cigar. He had not noticed how tall he was before. And his cigar was strangely potent.

Now was not the time to address him. That much was clear when the eyes followed him as Silence passed him.

Silence not only wanted to know him, he needed to know who he was as well.

He definitely looked familiar. But he could not place him or his name. He had no idea how long ago he may have seen him, but it was not a warm feeling.

He had surmised hours ago that they were both watching the same house from different corners. And that placed him on a very short list. He was either a friend or a foe. And the look on his face as he walked past him was far less than friendly.

The story the Marquess of Tisdale shared the next morning was rehearsed, but mercifully truthful. Kenneth had been getting used to no headaches. After all, he had spent all his waking time that he wasn't investigating seeing to it that the Hughes ladies had all they needed and updating the duke. So even a bit of shadiness in a truth was painfully noticed.

He appreciated Evelyn's beautifully honest, truthful side.

And all the other beautiful sides as well.

Reminding himself that he was reviewing the facts he knew so far, he continued ruminating on his early meetings after the return to London.

The ride the next morning was a wet one. It was unfortunate that it was raining, but three times the marquess declined the chance to wait it out in a café. Instead, the disclosure occurred in the rain.

"It is more private than White's," he'd said when Silence suggested it to him.

The recommendation to try the café with Italian ice was declined with a simple, "No thank you."

It was true, Italian ice was not all that alluring when your great coat was failing to prevent the elements from affecting his person.

But the request made by Silence to stop for a pint, or even imbibe this early, was also refused. "I have brandy at home that can warm me later. If you do not mind, let us proceed."

They finally stopped at the intersection of Fame, Greed, Honor, and Filth. Ironically, they had entered by way of Honor.

With all the comings and goings that usually occurred at this intersection, the rain had a unique talent of drowning out their voices to those in carriages passing them.

Grey was correct; this was far more private.

The Marquess of Tisdale started to share what he knew, but the first sentences turned out to be the most shocking. "My uncle is still alive. The one I inherited my title from. I am not rightfully the marquess."

*****

Silence pondered that conversation over and over again. All that Grey had told him that rainy morning had been entirely true; he had felt it deep in his cold, shivering bones.

He began to list the facts that he learned in the rain.

Grey was looking for the ladies.

And he was not the rightful marquess.

The uncle had been in touch with Grey and was demanding to know where Evelyn and Ester were.

Grey had wanted to marry Miss Evelyn Hughes, and had been planning to propose the next day after the Halliburtons' dinner party.

And strangely, he asked about Honeymae, stating that he had trained the dog to like him with small treats from his pocket.

Why did Grey ask about the English Mastiff?

Did his training of the dog mean anything? He felt like it had. Like the marquess was apologizing, or confessing, but there was no harm in making your future wife's dog adore you.

And where was the uncle?

He had a strong suspicion that the man smoking the cigar was the true marquess.

"Silence? Am I interrupting you and your book?" Evelyn asked timidly.

He stood up, closed his book he wasn't reading, and bowed. "No, you are never unwelcome. Are you enjoying this glorious late summer weather?"

She smiled and queried, "How are you? The cook says you did not take your breakfast in your room, as I had assumed. Are you unwell?"

He wondered at how thoughtful Evelyn Hughes was; how wrong he was to have ever thought she was selfish. She was willing to do anything for those who had earned her trust. He dared to hope that she felt more than trust for him. He never had headaches around her, and lately there had been no heated arguments, but plenty of private rendezvous that led to a stolen kiss or two. Perhaps a bit more than two.

"Thank you but no, Miss Hughes, I would say I am not unwell."

"But you would not say you are well." She cleared her throat, and in a mock Irish accent hooted, "Ye have the look of a carpenter ready to whittle without 'is tools."

His angst lifted momentarily chuckling, and he added with his own terrible brogue, "Thank ye, kindly." Which sent them both into hysterics.

After a moment she paused in her own glorious laughter, and her countenance sobered. She must have sensed his discontent, and was waiting for him to ask her to help him.

He complied, but reluctantly. After all, what kind of investigator asks others for help?

"Here is what I know. The true marquess faked his own death to get out of a badly played hand of cards or, actually, a duel with his own brother. As you know, Harrison's father was killed in that duel. But Charles Grey was a card sharp and knew how to double his earnings—not to mention the land and estates brought in over twelve-thousand pounds a year. So money was not in short supply. Why would he give it all up? Which makes me think he was—"

"Afraid, perhaps even for his life," she finished for him.

Silence simply nodded. "At least desperate enough to run from someone who had suspicions about the death of Lord William Grey."

"We also know that when his state of health, not death, was discovered by his nephew, Mr. Harrison Grey, your previous suitor, that it was handled secretly. All of society still believes the true marquess is deceased, and that Harrison Grey inherited. But Grey is asking me to help find *you*. The connection was simple enough to presume. As I told you, I believe the bet your father made of the marriage of his firstborn was made to Mr. Charles Grey, the uncle in hiding. He was single, had no heir, and enjoyed the tables."

When he didn't say anything for an extended minute, she placed a gentle hand on his elbow. "Kenneth, you need to step out of your head. Either that, or let me into yours. I wish to help you in any way I can."

He placed his hand on the one she had placed on his arm. Then picked it up deliberately, lifting it to his mouth. He bowed over it, enough to smell her fragrance; it smelled of vanilla bean and churned caramel. The scent made the perfect permanent memory in his heart.

He sealed that memory with a kiss to the back of her hand, then the back of her wrist. He had only done this one other time, yesterday, in fact, but the effect on her then was a glorious drunken look in her eyes afterwards.

He heard her whisper breathlessly, "You would not dare . . ." The pleading and hope dripped like sap from her voice. But she still glanced around the garden to make sure they were alone again.

Oh, he dared.

He kissed the back of her wrist again, his breathing caressing the forearm. Higher. First with his still lips, then with tender kisses, leaving her in anticipation of when and where the next kiss would land. He explored her entire arm with wandering lips.

Her breathing increased in rate and depth, encouraging him further. He breathed on her arm when she wanted kisses, kissed when she had given up hope that he would, and paused when she moved to communicate she wanted more.

Then, finally, he hungrily pulled her close.

The desire had been intense these last few weeks, being under the same roof. The pull was building with each curiously secluded discussion they found themselves in.

But when they found themselves not together, the longing rose until they found each other. To be alone meant desire to be closer than propriety allowed. But being together created a magnetic energy, vibrating between them as tangibly as the cloth his clothes were made of.

He could touch it.

And at the moment, he actually was.

He continued to ponder how this moment came to be.

Eventually, that magnetic energy was acknowledged. It only took a few days to lose proper host versus guest relations.

Never would he have ever dared to steal even a few kisses from a guest of his house, but she had a way of pressing him to do what is not what he had always done.

Once they kissed again, the expectation of connecting with her lips would lift the hair on the back of his neck in a way he craved.

He knew why he craved her. Kenneth Silence was in love.

And even though he could not say it yet, denying the truth was not in his character.

But could he? Could he express that love?

He placed her arm that he was making love to around his own neck, and she complied immediately in caressing his hair that had grown just long enough to feather around his ears.

Silence held that petite waist in both hands, daring to let them drift low enough to feel the beginning of the feminine waistline built into what made a woman a woman. He then returned them to her narrow waist and leaned down, whispering, "Yes, Miss Evelyn Hughes I will kiss you, as you requested."

She almost had time for rebuttal, for they both knew she most definitely did not ask to be kissed. *At least not with words,* he thought.

She met him halfway and kissed him hungrily. Her lips, those precious tools she used to spar with him, communicated a mixture of love and war now. She, too, knew when to give and withhold, as he did with the kisses to her arm, based on Kenneth's own pleading lips.

Each time she pulled away he followed, which was met with an eventual priceless reward. The union of their lips built the intrinsic energy, as if a lantern had fallen in a cornfield.

What was nonverbally asked for was eventually given, but not immediately; it was delayed gratification in the most sensual form. She leaned in, only for him to parallel her movement and then greedily reward her expressions of desire.

Their hands wanted more but neither had dared, so far, to do anything more than pull and caress his shoulders, and the same for him with the small of her back and the swell of her hips.

She had the perfect hourglass figure, and during the summer had bronzed a bit with the summer sun when she lived in the cottage. But after three weeks the skin had lightened, the calluses on her hands had softened, and so had she.

They no longer bitterly fought, but instead flirted with their wits, which he suspected was how it had been from the beginning.

They were fire and water, the two of them. They were kindling to the inner spirits, each one encouraging the innate identity that so much of society hammers out of favor. He was not the same as her, but his differences strengthened her. He was not perfect, no, but she was the perfect cure for his drawbacks and frailties.

She would push him, even irritate and rub him in just the right way, as a jeweler were to polish a precious gem.

Evelyn started to pull away and he reluctantly complied, stepping away just enough to look down into her blue eyes. "Do you know . . ." He paused to take a breath. He had not mastered his breathing yet from their kisses. "Do you know what a soul mate is?"

It was the closest he had come to declaring himself. He was ready, and prayed she was, too.

Hope flashed in her eyes, and she smiled. "It is someone who matches you entirely. The person you are destined to be with because they are the same as you."

"Oh, my dear, that is the traditional, fairytale definition. Let me share with you what a soul mate is, for once again you are *wrong*." He said the last part very facetiously.

Silence pulled away just in time to avoid the swat to the head. But he caught her right arm and kissed the hand once, tenderly. Then he looked for the left one and cradled them both in his hands as one.

He gazed up from the bundle of intertwined fingers and looked into her eyes. "Dear, sweet Evelyn, a soul mate is one who sees you for who you are, the good, and the bad, and presses you to be better. And in fact, helps you become your own destined potential. They are not usually the same as you. A soul mate can even be your friend, or your sister, if they challenge you to be better today than you were yesterday. They know what you are capable of, and spur you in that direction constantly, maybe even when you do not desire it or believe you can. They make you everything you are meant to be."

Silence had to stop for a brief moment and collect himself. The intensity and power of what he was about to do was evident, and he saw that she knew it, too. He had wanted her as his wife for far longer than he cared to admit, but now was the moment he would hear what level of devotion she had for him.

He prayed her heart surrendered to his, just as his had to hers.

"Miss Evelyn Hughes, dare I ask if you would take up swords with me and battle me daily, until I am everything I am capable of becoming, however long that might be? Will you correct my wrong moves, only to teach me to hit the target correctly, blindfolded, the next time I attempt it? And can I trust that you will hold me tight when I want to push away? But you must be willing to push me past my self-imposed limitations with love and kindness, gentleness and understanding. I ask you, dear Evelyn, to be the other half of my soul—to unite your soul, forever, with mine—and be my one true friend who will never agree for agreement's sake."

He continued, "But I plead with you to love me with your entire person, for your soul feels familiar, or kin to mine, and I know it has felt this way for ages. Frankly, your soul fixes the broken pieces of mine."

Stepping back with one foot, and while still grasping both of her hands, he knelt down and declared, "I love you, Miss Evelyn Hughes. Build me into that man you currently see behind my eyes. Marry me, and let us lengthen our relationship into forever, as soul mates."

Her smile widened, and she reached for his jaw gently with one hand then brushed his hair from his brow thoughtfully. Looking lovingly into his eyes, she said, "If that is what a soul mate is, then I gladly accept the compliment. I will be your soul mate, as long as you always look at me this way. No matter how our young babies may change my form or age pulls on my skin, you must always see the person you see right now, as well as always see my potential. For I, too, am quite confident you see more than I currently am, and I love you for that, with all my heart. I have no greater desire than to be everything you see I can be, with you forever."

CHAPTER 16

Once again she had been sufficiently distracted by his tenderness, a tenderness that she would have never known if it wasn't for her stay on the duke's land. It was a tenderness she would have never experienced if it were not for asking for Silence's help. She had only been rescued because of his powerful constitution to stand up to the forces of society that told him all the rumors about her.

Apparently there were a few rumors worse than a lady dressed as a man to go to university. There were some that assumed that she had fled to bear a child privately! The mortification of what that meant, to be exposed or ridiculed without being able to defend herself, had, at times, left her feeling fragile.

But he gave her strength that even she did not learn from being at the cottage. And she had every hope that by hiring Silence, she and her sister Ester would be free to return to society and safely be themselves.

True, no money would be exchanged, but she had bought what he was selling: his character, his wit, his heart, his love.

It was as if she and her family had been saved, just like in the Bible when Esther had approached the king to bravely reveal that she was a Jew, and in doing so saved them. If she had not done so, approached the king and asked for his help, then the proclamation to kill her family would have been passed.

She should think on that later, but for now she was in the embrace of her intended. She had not had such pleasure from touch before.

So few in society touch; even when ladies are together, they do not embrace often. Parents are taught to get nursemaids and keep the children in the nursery. She did not want that in her marriage. She wanted the children to be loved and kissed and tickled until they cried. She wanted lively interaction, and competitions over the smallest things, for she found delight in the fight for joy. In fact, she doubted she would have fallen for one who pampered her and minced words around her.

He had taken her hand and started leading her to the bench. "Why did you fall in love with me?" she asked.

"You spoke the truth, no matter how ugly it was."

"How curious an answer! I struggle with a retort."

"It is beautiful and freeing to *say* what is on one's mind, but even better to *hear* what is on another's mind. No matter how you abused me, or squared your shoulders stubbornly, you meant what you said. That is how trust is built, and from trust comes affection. Apparently your truthful nature endeared me to you quickly."

She took a seat on the bench he had gestured to. She giggled slightly, raised her eyebrow and flirted, "My duty as an elitist in society is complete! You have fallen for me, and I have ensnared you—and with all with the abuses and affronts of Shakespeare. You will never know the lies I have told you." Then she winked at him.

His brow furrowed a bit and she worried that he actually doubted her nature. He sat down next to her.

"Dear Silence, I was only teasing. I have never told you a lie; at least not intentionally."

"I know. I definitely know that." He stood from the bench, almost as quickly as he had sat down. She looked at the seat to see if maybe his side had been wet to explain his sudden fidgeting and straightening of his coattails.

"You do? You 'definitely know' that I have not been lying to you?"

He looked up, but his eyes looked . . . sad? No. Guilty.

She stood, too, and he motioned for her to sit back down.

Silence cleared his throat, then managed to croak out nervously, "I believe that, since I was a small child, I could discern right from wrong. Truth from error."

"Then you had excellent parents who taught you the ways of the Lord."

His gaze left hers for a little while and there seemed to be a depth to them, a distance, that she had never seen before. Whatever he was trying to tell her, it was important that she understand.

She placed her hand on the crook of his arm, and it had the intended effect on his person, bringing him from that foreign place to her presence again.

"Are you well? Kenneth, please, help me understand what you wish to tell me. It will not change my affection or my desire to marry you."

Simultaneously, his face relaxed into a soft smile while exhaling. "You mean it, Evelyn."

"You did not say that as a question, but of course I mean it."

"No, you see I know you mean it. I can feel it inside."

Her brow furrowed in confusion. But she decided she should just allow him to explain.

"I know when something is even a little wrong. Sometimes it is simply good intuition, other times it is like a punch in the gut that makes the falsehood known to me. Usually, though, it is the small changes in someone's character, or movements, or tone of voice. But no matter how obvious or subtle, it gives me a headache."

He mindlessly reached to his head and rubbed it, but proceeded to explain. "I know, without a doubt, if someone is lying. I know it on the inside, as surely as I would recognize my mother's face, or the taste of mint jelly. I have never been wrong. And, to make things worse for me . . ."

"Worse? Goodness! How can you say that? What a beautiful gift!"

He looked somewhat surprised by her radical acceptance, but he continued, hesitantly at first, then it all came out as a rush. "Yes, worse. You see, everyone lies; well, that is until I met you. *You* do not seem to lie. Either that or my 'gift', as you say, is muted drastically around you. Even your abuses and affronts, delivered in lines from hundreds of years ago, felt more true and natural than anything the *ton* serves at dinner parties. It is disheartening, let me tell you, how few people speak their mind. I had not noticed the first time I met you, but even then, when I heard your whispers of hoping to marry Mr. Grey, I did not sense any form of half-truth. It was all so beautifully choreographed. Your words come to my ears like oil to the spokes of a rusted wagon wheel. It soothes my heart, my mind, and therefore my head. I feel peace and a complete let down of my desire to perform as the flirtatious dandy that society knows me as. In fact, just before I met you, I had started my own form of rebellion against society."

"How so?" She had heard so much, but this last statement eliminated any other thought from her mind. For some reason, she wanted to know who Silence was prior to the one she fell in love with.

"Remember, you asked me a question. And I will honor you with the truth. I loved ladies, I loved admiring them, and most of all I loved that they admired me."

He had paused, but she dearly hoped he would continue and not notice the crimson heat rising in her cheeks. She did not know how she felt about knowing this about Silence.

She sighed, but then knew that he had never hidden anything from her. If she asked, he answered. He was a man who spoke the truth. It was up to her to accept any differences that they had.

There was so much to process all at once.

But then she saw in his eyes that he knew what she felt. That the moment she opened her mouth, he would know the truth of her shock.

She nodded briefly and said, "Of course you have. It is the way of our peers."

He also nodded, completely accepting the only answer she was ready to give. "Fortunately, my endurance ran out. I had given up hope, about three weeks before the Halliburtons' dinner party, that I would ever be rid of the headache. You have no idea how raw one's heart can get as they continually look for truth, only to feel the inconsistencies of what nearly everyone says abrade against what they actually believe or do."

"I can only imagine. And every lie causes a headache?"

"No, it is more the collection of them all. Like the Leaning Tower of Pisa, I imagine unstable foundations in everyone around me. I feel the danger, and the risk of disclosing who I am. My muscles tighten, my neck stiffens, and I get a headache."

It sounded so logical. All of it, from the inconsistent mannerisms he noticed, to the tone of voice, to the associated tension headaches. Somewhere deep in her soul, she understood that this was a deeply seated part of him that he desperately needed her to accept.

"I think I understand." And Evelyn did understand. "How long have you been aware of this gift? Who else knows?"

He chuckled, and shook his head in disbelief. "You are phenomenal. I truly believe the heaven and stars aligned in order to place us in each other's path."

"Kenneth, it is not too unlikely for two of the privileged *ton* to eventually meet. The Halliburtons have parties frequently. If we had not met there it would be another party, or at the theatre."

"Yes, and the Halliburtons are having another one in two days. But that is not the path I was referring to, my dear." He wiggled his eyebrows and winked, then claimed a small kiss on her cheek.

She smiled at him, and immediately was rewarded with his smile in return. "Yes, how unlikely that we would have met at the exact moment, and to have even recognized each other."

"You could have easily hidden your identity from me, but you did not. You were not dressed to your station, and yet you still allowed your face and identity to be discovered. I am ashamed to admit it, but I likely would have allowed a peasant to continue without so much as a by your leave. But your heated words, and pointed 'you will thank me someday', only brought attention to your class and education. For no peasant would have dared speak to a gentleman riding on the duke's land that way."

"Oh dear, you make me sound so uncouth."

"No, my love, your disgust for me was consistent with your words. I was like a moth to the flame from that very moment. You invaded the fabric of my sinews. It was rare that I even used my limbs without thinking about you. Even when I did nothing but sleep, you paraded your beauty throughout my dreams. I have never slept so well as I have these last few months. Dreams are the only interruption. And the only honest thing to admit is that I craved retiring, for I met with you often in that dreamworld. And soon, I shall never want to do anything other than have you lying next to me. I can never express how grateful I am for your kindness, and ready acceptance of what would be disturbing to most people."

A small part of her began to blush, hearing that he had been dreaming about her, but the words were said so plainly, so lovingly, so truthfully, that there was no need to be flattered or embarrassed. He was just expressing his love. And to have been trusted with this knowledge was unbelievable!

"Who else knows about your gift?" she asked.

"The duke and duchess do, and his brother, Spencer, did. But most of the others who knew are no longer alive. My father was one who, I believe, also had this gift, as did his father before him. But my father drowned it out with alcohol—rum, to be exact. To this day I cannot stand the sweet smell."

"Does it work? The alcohol? Does it numb the gift?"

"I am afraid it does, just as it numbs self-restraint, compassion, generosity, and respect in others you have associated with. That is why gambling and drinking usually go hand in hand."

Evelyn absorbed the first part of what he just said for a moment. ". . . numbs self-restraint," she repeated. "I understand and have seen that for myself. But how does alcohol numb generosity?"

"What is the opposite of generosity?"

A servant came and delivered a letter, and while she talked he read it.

She was clearly talking to herself. That is, until the end. "Ah-ha, I see now, the opposite of generosity is selfishness. But what about respect? Dishonor? Yes, that works as an opposite. How intriguing. This is a concept I have never pondered before. It places my father's bet in a new perspective. Do you know that he never drinks when gambling?"

He looked up, and nodded. "Now I do." Placing the note in his vest pocket, he gave her his full attention again.

She smiled. He could detect truth from lies. "He told me that, the night he made that disastrous bet, he chose to drink. That one of the men that night had a cider that was like drinking spiced apple pie. He said the drink was so strong it permeated the room, was admired and adored by all those in attendance. Everyone raved about it enough that he chose to drink."

"Spiced apple pie? A liquor?"

If she hadn't had his full attention before, now she did.

She nodded even though he hadn't asked in clarification, but as if he was processing or deciding how to explain what he had just learned.

She waited for him to expound why her father drinking a strong, spiced cider was curious or even continued to occupy his mind more than a second, but his mind was working so fast she didn't dare interrupt.

He stood and grasped his hands behind his back and began to pace from the Echinacea plants to the blue asters in the garden. He would slow his pace at times, but then proceed with passion a few seconds later.

Finally, he turned on his heel and faced her. "I think I shall reply to the Halliburtons' autumn masquerade invitation. It is time that we have you reenter society. But first, we inform your father that you are in town. It is time for you to return to your childhood home."

She stood quickly, "You would not put Ester in danger. Please say you will not."

"No, she will stay hidden; safely hidden with your mother and a few guards. How soon can you have a dress readied, to be presented as my intended to all of those in attendance? The dinner is in two days."

"I suppose if I have access to my lady's maid and my wardrobe at my father's house, with just enough time to prepare as I have in the past. A few hours."

His reaction was spontaneous, and yet so disbelieving that she giggled.

Silence spoke slowly, failing miserably at hiding his naivety of what it takes to look like a lady in today's society. "I understand that you will already have a gown, but why do you need a few hours to ready yourself?"

"A lady who has not been seen in society for many months has many rumors to put to rest in a single night. You would not have me look the part of a witch who makes love potions with moonbeams and turtle breath, would you? Now, forget the nonsensical questions. What is this plan you formed?"

"Oh, my dear Evelyn Hughes, I think I have it all puzzled out," he said, tapping the side pocket. "Now go and tell your sister that her husband will be here at my townhouse late tomorrow."

Evelyn stood quickly. "What? How did he know where we are?"

"I told you that I would be reading Phillip's letters to Ester. She expressed no hesitation in letting me, if it meant being reunited with him. I promised her that I would write him and alert him to the arson as well as that she is safe. You know time is running out for her; she will be in travail in a few short weeks at the least."

"Definitely. So you wrote him?"

"I did. I am surprised that I had not heard anything these last two weeks. However, it turns out that you offered one piece of the puzzle, while his letter," he patted the side pocket, "offered another. I do believe I have it now. Yes. I do believe that I know how to ensure Mr. Charles Grey is brought out into the light."

CHAPTER 17

Silence's plan needed to be fleshed out a bit, and there was little time to do it.

He had already met with Mr. Harrison Grey, and he knew his role to perform.

The next day, they arrived at Hughes House to share what part of the plan they could with Mr. and Mrs. Hughes. It had been a marvelous idea to send around Silence's card only ten minutes prior to arriving, because neither of them had time to alter their appearance or, if Silence was wrong, do something disastrous.

Both Mr. and Mrs. Hughes were ready and anxious to see their daughter with such short notice.

Mr. Hughes stood when they entered the room—unshaven, hair disheveled, and his face was pained. The emotion expressed was unrestrained from his face as relief and compassion mixed in one. He took long hustled strides and engulfed his second daughter in his arms. "You are safe. My dearest Evie, is it really you?" He held her tightly and kissed the top of her head several times.

Silence did not need the gift of discernment to know that this father had never known where his daughters had been, nor what elements they had been exposed to. He had been looking for them all this time, not to sell off his daughter but to protect her.

Mrs. Hughes was just as thrilled to embrace her favorite child, and the pure expression of longing when they were shown into the room was priceless.

She, too, was innocent, just as he suspected, yet she was the one who sent them away. It was done without her husband's knowledge, and from the looks of her worn dresses he assumed it was her pin money that was sent. Which she later confirmed.

She held Evelyn to her chest and sighed audibly. Then pulled away just enough to examine her quickly.

When the reunion was completed, and the words of love expressed, Mr. Hughes cleared his throat in a fatherly way, and found his manners. "Come in, come have a seat. You must be Mr. Silence."

"Mr. Kenneth Silence, at your service."

"Well, Silence, I understand from your note that Mr. Grey—er, the Marquess of Tisdale—hired you to find our daughters. All I own will be yours; you just name it. But tell me that Ester is safe. Do ease a father's heart."

Silence nodded with a warm smile. He especially liked that he hadn't said, "A father's *mind*". He had very accurately stated that his heart was uneasy while they were gone.

"Yes, Mr. Hughes, she is indeed safe. We have also heard from her husband yesterday, Mr. Phillip Thomas; he is expected later today as well. Are you aware that you may be welcoming a grandson or granddaughter into the world shortly?"

Her father looked to Evelyn, who had worn one of her more casual dresses, and she suddenly gasped beside him. "Not me, Father! I am not married yet!"

"My Ester is with child?" He hadn't yet sat down as the others in the room had, but found the need at that moment next to his wife.

His wife patted his knee and said, "Yes dear, her time is likely in the next month or less." She then turned back to her daughter. "How is she?"

Mr. Hughes turned to his wife. "How could you keep this from me?"

Evelyn defused the question with, "She is very well. Uncomfortable, hot, and tired, though."

Her mother began to grin widely, "Oh yes, I recall those last months. I dearly wish to see her. Please, take me to her."

Kenneth spoke up. "First, we need to disclose another upcoming celebration. Miss Evelyn Hughes has agreed to gift her life to me as my wife. And I would have it no other way but to gift myself to her as her husband."

The mood in the room darkened significantly.

This was just as he had expected, and planned.

"But . . ." her mother said.

"It is not possible . . . the bet . . ." said her father.

"It is," Evelyn assured. "Put your trust in us. We need to be sure of a few things first."

He stuttered slightly, but then nodded vigorously. "Yes, yes of course. I have the greatest regret in all that has occurred. I should have let Ester marry who she desired. I have heard many wondrous things about you, Silence, and I know you will help us find peace with what has occurred. Your note states that you are aware of the unfortunate bet I made years ago when they were eight years old." The guilt was thick in his voice.

"Yes, sir. And as I had mentioned earlier, I am also aware that Mr. and Mrs. Phillips eloped to Gretna Green, eliminating her as a candidate for making good on that bet. Which leaves my intended, who I might remind you is of age. I have to ask you, Mr. Hughes, if I am looking for the right man. I understand that the Marquess of Tisdale is the man you made the bet with."

"The former marquess, not his nephew who courted my daughter. Mr. Grey is the nephew of the putrid man."

Evelyn looked at Silence quickly, and Silence nodded. "I met Mr. Greys' father, the brother to the man you made the bet with, and he had a unique smell, too. I would say the Tisdale family all have a bit of a musk, or odor to them. But I cannot place why. It is cloves and an array of spices, that much I know."

Mrs. Hughes shared, "Four generations ago, the marquess married a peasant girl whose father had worked in an apothecary's office. Myth says she was a witch, and made potions. But she found a mixture of herbs and spices that, when mixed with a bit of buttermilk from goats, became extremely useful in controlling hair when used as a pomade, as well as hair dandruff, which they were all afflicted with. It became favored in society in the mid-18th-century momentarily. However, when the less potent pomades were discovered, the clove-based one no longer was used among society. Tradition is tradition, I suppose. The whole family has used the pomade for as long as I can remember."

"Including Mr. Charles Grey, the Marquess of Tisdale's uncle?"

"Oh yes, he reeked of it," Mrs. Hughes said. "Are we allowed to ask why you are asking about the previous marquess? Or the pomade?"

"We believe that he is involved with a recent act of arson inflicted on the duke's land."

Mrs. Hughes gasped. "He could not! Not my girls! Where is Ester? I demand to see her!" She stood and Evelyn went and comforted her mother with gentle hands.

"Mother, please, as much as you begged me to trust you all of these months, you must trust us now. She is unharmed and happy. She is so very happy now that she knows her Phillip will be here. We expect him very soon."

There was only a second of stillness in the air after Mrs. Hughes was guided to sit back down when Mr. Hughes repositioned himself to the edge of his seat. "You said 'recent' arson. Surely you do not mean he is still alive?"

Silence stated, "For the safety of your daughters, this must remain confidential. But yes, we do. But considering one daughter is married, and since yesterday Evelyn is now betrothed to me, we must now focus our attention on flushing him out of hiding. Because the bet cannot be paid, unless you have other daughters I do not know of." He shook his head. "And I think I know how to flush him out."

"You will not, for I will knock you to your knees if you use my daughter as bait. I just got her back. You do not know how hard it was to have them away from me. You cannot understand, as you are not a mother," Mrs. Hughes informed him quite forcefully.

It was expected, this protective, mama-bear instinct to protect her cubs. Her jaw was set and she had now placed a protective arm around her only offspring in the room. If Silence's flesh could have melted, it would have with the look she was giving him.

He smiled warmly at her and waited.

"Momma, trust Silence; it is not me he intends to use as bait, but himself. You see, I will stay here, and Silence will be about town asking questions; very obvious questions about the previous marquess, to stir up suspicion among the peers that he is still alive. We are confident that he will come out of hiding and seek Silence out."

"And in my gossiping crusade, I will also let it slip that I have been hired by the current Mr. Grey to find someone important to him. You see, Mr. Grey, whom the elite know as the new Marquess of Tisdale, has been looking for your girls, too. But not for the reasons that might be suspected. He hired me some time ago to find them, stating that they were in danger. What I could never figure out was why he was so desperate to find them, besides keeping them from his uncle. Miss Hughes and I just left his home, and he was able to see Miss Hughes for the first time in ages. He congratulated us on our upcoming marriage, but then asked about Honeymae."

Both Silence and Evelyn looked at each other and laughed, but Silence explained. "It was ingenious of Mr. Grey back in December to have planned his proposal so creatively. However, timing did not pan out, as he was never readmitted at Hughes House the next morning after the Halliburtons' dinner party. We all know why."

Evelyn added, "Currently Honeymae is at the duke's townhouse, Willsing Manor, but in the collar around her neck is a pocket holding a three-carat diamond ring and a leather punched tag that says, 'Color my world, Marry me —Grey'."

"It was his grandmother's ring," Evelyn continued. "And when rumors erupted that I had gone to the country in a delicate condition, he simply wanted his grandmother's ring back. His grandmother is still alive, and can be a force to be reckoned with, enough to encourage Mr. Grey to hunt down Silence to find me, and Honeymae. He was too embarrassed to mention the ring and dog earlier. But he knew that she is usually with me."

"So that is why he continues to come calling? I assumed he was still moonstruck."

"But it is more than that, I am afraid," Silence explained. "His uncle is here, in London, and has been contacted. It happened two weeks ago. I actually came upon him as he was smoking his cigar."

"How did you know it was him?"

"I followed Grey and saw as he messaged someone by way of a street lad. But I followed Grey back home. I stayed several hours watching the house from afar, assuming someone would come, or at least Grey would leave to meet them. At this point in time I fully suspected Mr. Harrison Grey was the arsonist, you see, as he was the one who was known to have looked for them. The true marquess, Mr. Charles Grey, apparently had been summoned through that note, but saw me watching the house. I have never met Charles, but I met his brother when he was alive and there are great similarities, not to mention the smell of the cloves in the pomade. He was too suspicious to enter his nephew's house with me watching. The meeting never happened, nor was it rescheduled."

Both the Hugheses looked at each other nervously, and Mr. Hughes cleared his throat. "There has been a man observed loitering here around Hughes House for the last three months. I thought nothing of it because nothing has gone missing, and no one has been harmed. Could I have put us in harm's way but my unthinking ways?"

Evelyn patted her mother's knee and said to her father, "No, we do not think so. We assumed he was trying to find us, and likely took action in seeking us out. However, we have Mr. Harrison Grey's full cooperation. He summoned his uncle through the same street boy, and is meeting with him now, setting things up for tomorrow. There is no way he saw us arrive at Hughes House."

"Tomorrow? Oh, dear. What . . ."

"Have you by chance received an invitation to the Halliburtons' Autumn Masquerade?"

Both nodded.

"Good. Then we are all set. I will need Mrs. Hughes to stay with Ester, and Mr. Hughes to escort Miss Evelyn to the

Masquerade. Harrison will inform Charles that I will be there, wearing all black and white. This will make Charles Grey find me. This is where we will find and apprehend him. He is under the impression that I have found your daughters, but he will not know where they are."

"Silence, may I say something? It is very important to me."

"Of course, Mr. Hughes."

Her father looked to his daughter first, then back to Silence. "You are a man worthy of my daughter. I can see that. Your union has my blessing."

Silence nodded, a bit too tight in the chest with emotion to speak.

Evelyn spoke for him. "Thank you, Papa. He and I are united, but in the oddest of ways."

Mrs. Hughes asked in a strained voice, "Forgive me, but how did the marquess find our daughters? Was he the arsonist?"

"We will know tomorrow, God willing."

BUYING THE DUKE'S SILENCE

204

CHAPTER 18

The music was hypnotizing. Evelyn couldn't help but feel the music from Luigi Buccarini fill her soul. Jane Hadlock had a way of expressing the soul of a cello, and performing the works of the Italian composer put her at ease. Music in general had been nonexistent for her for the last almost eight months.

She tried to focus on the tasks at hand which were few, but important.

Everyone was in masks. Jane Hadlock was one of the only people she recognized because, in order to perform on the cello, she had to remove her blue and green peacock mask. Occasionally she felt the familiarity of a friend or two, but it wasn't until Silence entered, face simply painted, without a mask, that she found her ease.

She found it interesting that he came without a mask. It was likely for the same reason Jane took her mask off: he needed to see.

She watched from afar for over ten minutes. He wasn't looking for anyone in particular, but rather everyone. It was an interesting experience to watch him circle the room, scoping out the dangers, the exits, and those who might be foes, all while greeting those around him, complimenting the costumes or masks.

She performed her roll with ease, for she had been trained well in dancing and music. If Evelyn was asked to dance, she agreed. She was to act as if she had never left society.

Having Silence leave her with her parents yesterday night was terrifying. But she had done harder things. Not to mention that Ester arrived shortly after with her husband. Ester hadn't let go of Phillip's arm for hours. And when they retired early, no one blamed them. Phillip was completely solicitous to her sister's care. For the first time in ages, she felt the mantle of responsibility lift.

After three dances, and two thirds of her dance card filled, her father checked in on her. They were not to be seen together, so she whispered to him while turned away, "I am well. Thank you. I always wanted to be seen at parties like this. It is strangely comforting to be hidden behind the mask of Cleopatra." It was a good choice, because that meant she had to wear a black wig. Her recognizable red hair would have disclosed her identity.

"May I have the next dance?" The voice came from behind and was low to her ear. Comfort filled her bosom. It was clear who it was.

She turned towards Silence, but not before she saw a proud smile lighten her father's face.

There Kenneth was, also grinning from ear to ear. His face was painted like a Chinese yin-yang, his chin was painted black with a white dot, and the curved paint wrapped to his forehead and came to a point at his scalp. The white paint wrapped from forehead down to the jaw on the right. His clothing was entirely black and white. A white, two-toned vest, a black cravat, and a black tailcoat, black trousers that his valet had sewn white ribbons down the sides, white socks, and black dancing shoes made up his entire wardrobe.

And she could not gather herself enough to stop thinking how handsome he was. His hair, which usually had a bit of wave to it, now had more prominent curls that seemed to shine more than usual.

"You amaze me," he whispered.

He took her hand and guided her to the dancefloor.

"Do you presume that I would say yes to your request? I have not even checked my dance card. You would not dare assume my acceptance." She of course was sparring with him as usual, for she desperately wanted to dance with him.

He continued in his desire towards the front of the dance line. They were in position one, which meant, as the song progressed, the dance would take them down the line, promenading and turning as the steps demanded.

Silence must have picked this particular dance for a reason. Conversation was easy when your neighbor continued to move up the line, while you progressed down the line.

"Oh I dare, my queen. You are rising quickly to power over me."

Somehow, she had no desire to fight or abuse. Not tonight. Tonight there was a union of purpose. She had an advocate, not an adversary. She desired to tell him that.

Heat was rising in her cheeks and she knew a blush was apparent.

"Is there something the matter?" he whispered.

"No, nothing at all."

He reached for her hand to pull her towards him for the turn and whispered the words of Shakespeare's 138th sonnet: "'When my love swears that she is made of truth, I do believe her, though I know she lies.'"

She couldn't help but smile. Dare she quote love sonnets while dancing in public?

She started to share one of her favorites, but they separated, and then she lost her nerve.

Silence was too quick: "'My tongue-tied Muse in manners holds her still.'" It was the 85th sonnet.

The pull to declare her feelings, in light that they were to hide their engagement until later, was wickedly tempting, and daunting.

Her cheeks flushed scarlet again, and of course he delivered his third line, this one perfectly chosen from the 82nd sonnet:

"'Where cheeks need blood; in thee it is abus'd'." His eyes begged her to participate, laced with compassion for her plight and longing from being separated for the last day.

It appeared that he wished to stay in the sonnets, and she could think of nothing other than how she had an advocate and not an adversary again. "My thoughts were more along the line of the 36th sonnet: 'Let me confess that we two must be twain, although our undivided loves are one.' I must admit 'though our lives a separable spite, which though it alter not love's sole effect'."

He started to step forward at the wrong time of the dance and she shook her head, smiling when he rolled his eyes and mocked himself for making the mistake. Was he just performing his role as dandy or jester?

She then pretended to try to teach him the next steps. They had been performing them flawlessly and were nearly at the end of the line. And when it was time to grasp hands again and turn, she gave him a subtle wink.

He smiled widely and, with some subtle additional pauses, made the 88th sonnet work for them. "'That, for thy right, myself will bear all wrong.' Miss Hughes, you look beautiful tonight. I only reached from the sonnets because, surprisingly, I could not find the right words to express how right it is to see you in your proper station. You shine in the role that is rightfully yours."

"I shine, dear Silence, because of your affection and trust in me."

"It is you who trusts in me."

She leaned in and whispered, "Is he here?"

"I believe so. I have not had the confirmation yet, but I was able to locate Harrison Grey; he has on a full mask of a lion. I only found him because of the cloves and height. There are two other men as tall as him, but they seem to be moving just out of reach for me to detect the spicy pomade. I will give you a signal when it is time. And you must leave immediately."

"I know. Are you nervous?"

"I would not say that; however, I am having second thoughts about having you here. It was unnecessary."

"But I insisted." Which he already knew.

The music ended, and they bowed to each other. But just as he lifted his gaze, he halted and stared past her left shoulder. In a barely audible whisper he said, "Go. Go now."

She curtsied and did as she was told.

Resisting the urge to look over her left shoulder, she returned to the refreshment table where she was required to stay. Silence had arranged for the magistrate to be there, and if the gentleman who was cleverly, but conspicuously, dressed as a constable was the magistrate, then she knew who to discuss things with.

He had a hat low to his face, but a single eyeglass was decorated with colorful glass ornaments and a gaudy gold chain that distracted from others to take notice of his actual ruddy face. He must have had some difficulty with skin clarity in his youth, for there were deep pockmarks.

She smiled, more of an acknowledgement to the magistrate in helping her and Silence bring justice to the real marquess and he tipped his hat, confirming his identity.

She hadn't thought the magistrate all that tall until another gentleman, also with an eyeglass, dressed as a court jester with his shoe untied, walked past, pretending to trip. She got a small whiff of cloves and stepped closer to the magistrate with the eyeglass. Dancing with Silence had lightened the mood a great deal.

She refocused her attention on the task at hand. She scanned for Silence and saw him watching her.

The magistrate wasn't very young either, and likely why he was considered mature enough to be the magistrate.

He was broad-shouldered, but years of deskwork made his shoulders slump slightly. Either that or it was the role he was performing at the masquerade. It was more likely the former.

She was about a meter away from the magistrate when she saw Silence from much further away tilt his head sharply towards the man on her right, the Jester.

She whispered, "I know," to him, trying not to laugh. When the jester bent down to tie the shoe, he also dropped his eyeglass. She looked up at Silence who had rolled his eyes, making a drinking gesture, as if the jester was foxed, but then he pointed towards the punch bowl.

She doubted the jester was in his cups, but she did think he was playing the role nicely.

Looking back at the magistrate, who just put down his cup by the punch bowl, she saw him observing her. She smiled again, and he must have taken that as an invitation to approach.

It wasn't in the plan, but it wouldn't have been unwelcome.

"Good evening," she said. "Are you who I think you are?"

"I can be. Who do you want me to be?"

She furrowed her brow in confusion at the response, but looked up at him. It was then that she saw the jet-black hair on the side of his hat, slicked back.

Immediately she took a breath through her nose, but she need not smell the cloves to confirm that it was Charles Grey, the uncle. She had a wonderful perspective of the jet-black eyes. They held equal parts greed and lust.

With no effort from him, but all the effort she could muster to resist, he was ushering her towards the side of the room. She could have been made of straw, he moved her so easily.

Her heart pounded in her chest and she readied herself to fight; stomp on his foot, drive her elbow into his side, or scratch at the hand that gripped her arm with fervor.

But his cold words silenced her.

"Mrs. Ester *Thomas* is safe . . . for now." He had hissed the last name of her dear sister whom she had strived to protect for months. "Come now, come with haste. I refuse to have my bride be bruised and battered." His hearty laugh made her shudder.

She looked behind her frantically but saw no one but her captor, the marquess. He was everywhere. He was big enough to be three of her frame, and a few hands taller than her, too. He definitely was no longer slouching and she understood just how big he was. The smell of cloves this close was sickening, almost to the point of choking her.

She couldn't understand why Silence hadn't already intervened. But she realized his body not only moved her forward, but must have hid her entirely from the room. She knew she had to have her hands free, so she dropped her dance card and reticule, nearly tripping on it as it fell to the ground. But she managed to call out, "Silence!"

She ripped off her mask and threw it to the ground. She needed to see. Charles Grey pushed her into a narrow doorway to the left, not much bigger than a servant's passageway. It appeared that no one had entered the hallway for some time, as there were dust and spider webs in every nook.

The hall was not wide, and its ceiling was not very accommodating of Charles Grey. He was forced to stretch his arm out a bit, the one holding her as well as pushing her, in order to stoop under the beams that hung too low for him. It seemed that the pitch was shortening, too.

There was a small window at the end, only a few meters away, high above them in the unfinished rafters. It allowed them light to see where they were going. There were only a few low beams left before it would open up into a higher-peaked gable where the window was framed. His grip was making the beads of her dress fall to the floor.

Little by little she widened the distance between him until, with the final pitch of the hallway, she pulled out of his grip and darted to the left part of the hallway's fork. She heard the sound of beads falling all around, and even stepped on them with her dancing slippers.

Her slippers had no grip, and there was plenty of dust and warped boards to make a true sprint unsafe, but she did her best.

Sometimes, at the most opportune times, one is given thoughts that are not their own. She heard Eddie's Irish brogue in her head as he said, *"May you have the hindsight to know where you have been, the foresight to know where you are going, and the insight to know when you have gone too far."*

She stopped. If felt like more than a saying. For once, she actually got the words right in her head. Silence was right—she was always getting the sayings wrong.

But she chose to listen to that still, small voice that had kept her company all those lonely months; protecting her, caring for her, and comforting her at the darkest times.

"Insight to know when you have gone too far . . ." She heard in her head again.

Immediately, she turned around and she saw it—a very narrow door. A door fit for a child.

Thank you, Eddie!

She attempted to open it then saw the offending single hook-and-eye lock on it towards the top and managed to lift it quickly. Sliding through she came out behind some heavy draperies, ripping the hem of her Cleopatra dress on a warped, splintered board.

She gave no thought to it until it was time to reenter the ballroom to find Silence. She waited behind the drapes, wondering what to do next. The distant noise was easily the ballroom, but she was so shaken she almost couldn't proceed. It was very unlikely that Charles Grey could fit through the child's doorway, but she did not want to stay and find out.

The beads of her Egyptian dress were dropping quickly as she moved further and further towards the noise of the ballroom.

She took a breath and took several steps into the ballroom, searching for Silence.

There could not be a better comfort than the sound of the ballroom and the laughter of its occupants.

That is until the sounds changed from laughter to gasps, followed by the entire room's conversations hushed. She knew she was a sight, tattered a bit and filthy from head to toe. She knew at least one of her hairpins had snagged on the rafters as she ducked under them.

There were more important things than what society thought.

"Help me! I need Kenneth Silence!" She had found her voice and, gratefully, her voice had found Silence.

"Here!" His long strides were only slowed by his attempt to remove his black tailcoat while walking at such speed. He embraced her tightly.

Kenneth Silence then put the coat around Evelyn's shoulders. "The magistrate and I followed after you. We found a dance card, a reticule, plenty of beads, and very small footprints leading to the door. We could not get through it, though. But we have Charles Grey in custody. How did you escape?"

"Eddie showed me the way out."

Silence raised an eyebrow curiously and just embraced her again, saying, "You can tell me another time."

Another masculine voice interrupted. "Miss Hughes? Forgive me, but can we take this into another room? Your intended, Mr. Silence, has some accusations that you and your father will need to confirm with me."

The gentleman whom she had assumed was a clumsy jester was actually the real magistrate. She had gotten them mixed up, thinking Silence had indicated to the jester as being a fool and not indicating the man who eventually abducted her was actually Charles Grey.

"He has Ester!" Evelyn cried.

"Be calm, Evelyn, everything is well."

"What? How can everything be well? He says that he has Ester!"

"Exactly. He told me that, too, but he was *lying*."

She paused momentarily in walking and half-smiled. How she was going to love being married to the man who could discern all things.

He knew the truth. He was never wrong. Charles Grey had been bluffing. Relief flooded her body.

She had never been more grateful for Silence in the room at that moment.

"Thank you." She could barely put any strength to the breathy words.

He smiled wickedly and said, "I told you that you would 'thank me someday' for what happened in this room."

CHAPTER 19

Silence had summarized it already for Evelyn in the carriage, but had to retell it to Mr. and Mrs. Hughes, with Ester and Phillip listening.

"Phillip's letter confirmed it for me. He had a very nosy shipmate named Jacobson, who went by Jacobs. Ester had sent a letter with the actual direction on the letter, rather than diverting it through her mother. As you know all mail was sent through her, and she directed it to the duke. However, in a moment of weakness, Miss Ester, forgive me, Mrs. Thomas, wrote directly from the cottage.

"Knowing that Mr. Thomas and Ester had been close prior to the disappearance from society, Charles Grey was intelligent enough to track down Mr. Thomas first. It was not hard to find someone who needed a bit of pocket money, and Jacobson was the man who succumbed. One of the other shipmates had tipped Phillip off that they had been approached, but declined. This put Phillip on alert, but it was too late. Once the letter with the address was stolen, and found on Jacobson, he was arrested.

"Phillip's letter indicated such, and that he was accompanying Jacobson to the local constable here in London, where he confessed that a man with pockmarks on his face and who smelled strongly of cloves had hired him to investigate the private affairs of Phillip Thomas."

The room was listening intently, so he explained his own role in raising the marquess from the dead. "I had to spread rumors in order to flush out the marquess. Harrison Grey and I met openly, while walking down the street. We did not lower our voices as he declared that he would pay anything to find this person who he cared for. How he worried for his very title, which may not be rightfully his. How he suspected from the very beginning that foul play was at hand in his father's death. He was an excellent sport, mixing the pronouns just enough so that the rumors could have been hiring me to find your daughter, and raise suspicion that his title was not as it seemed."

He continued, "As you know, Harrison Grey had learned of the bet, and asked many, many questions of others in society these many months. For he wanted to understand the gaming habits of his uncle, as well as find his grandmother's ring. So the rumors were easily believed, no matter which person they thought I was hired to look for.

"However, he was not the only man on the street who smelled of cloves. Both of the Greys, being tall in stature and smelling of cloves, were easily mistaken. And the lad from the street mistook Harrison for the more dangerous uncle. This is where he first learned of his uncle being alive. The boy confessed everything he had been hired to do by the uncle and basically was a double agent for Harrison.

"This is not, of course, how he first learned of the bet. It is noble of Harrison to do what he did when he found out about the bet," Silence stated.

"Yes, it was," Evelyn added.

"Harrison Grey learned almost immediately of the bet, because in going through his uncle's estate he found the document indicating the promise of your daughter, Mr. Hughes."

Mr. Hughes sat forward. "He actually still has the document?"

"No, I have the document. Harrison gave it to me, and now I give it to you." He reached into his coat pocket and offered it to the man.

"There is no document."

Silence felt a heavy twinge of pain but then he understood what Mr. Hughes had meant, and the pain abated.

Mr. Hughes took it and walked three steps to the left and tossed it in the fire. "There is *no longer* a document," he restated.

"Indeed, once he found the document Harrison chose to court Miss Hughes himself. His original plan was to become acquainted and then disclose the document to her. But he quickly began to admire her. Genuinely admire her. Considering her dog was protective, even interfering, he quickly started carrying treats in his trousers. Honeymae is easily trained, and loyal to those who have a dusting of dried meat in their pockets."

The room laughed and nodded in agreement, and he let them before proceeding.

He was about to speak but Mrs. Hughes asked, "So is Jacobson how Mr. Charles Grey knew where my daughters were? Was the uncle the arsonist?"

"Unfortunately, yes. I will get there. Harrison Grey told me that he did not need to hunt down his uncle. Charles found Harrison because he had heard Harrison was looking for Evelyn. He made it sound as if he wanted to turn himself in, give up his title and confess to the death of his brother. He shared these things because he wrongly assumed they could team up and that Harrison wanted the lady, too, but Harrison just wanted the ring back. In disclosing why Harrison was looking for her, he innocently shared how he had trained and befriended the English Mastiff.

"It was not long after Jacobs disclosed the location of the Hughes sisters that he was in the countryside and had trained the dog. Once trained with food he was not considered a trespasser, so Honeymae barked no alert to the inhabitants of the cottage. He groomed the dog for just long enough to watch the comings and goings. He confessed that Eddie was quite the obstruction in getting close to Ester and Evelyn."

Ester cleared her throat, her voice coming out timid and confused. "Why set fire to the cottage if he wanted to find and marry Evelyn?"

"We do not think it was entirely intentional. No, he did not have good intentions; however, Eddie reported that he heard a noise, and got up to investigate. He did not get far, when he heard glass breaking right before he was hit from behind. We think Grey might have tripped, or perhaps dropped his lantern. But either way we cannot prove it was arson, as he could have tossed the lantern on the woodpile, too. Charles Grey claimed he lost sense when the fire started and was afraid that Eddie was an attacker. Of course he claimed self-defense; however, Eddie was hit twice. The second, we believe, was after he went down.

"Eddie will be able to identify him tomorrow when he arrives with Honeymae. I sent for him as soon as the puzzle came to together. But it will not be necessary, now that he tried to capture Evelyn. That alone will send him to prison for life. And I am a bit grateful that it happened, for now he made for a solid case."

Of course this caused the room to erupt in gasps. Silence cringed inside and thought to himself: *Maybe there is a time and place to only tell part of the truth.*

"Your daughter was never in any danger. She very cleverly left us a beautiful trail of her belongings and beads. But it was unnecessary, considering that Charles Grey's stench could have been followed by a blind hunting dog.

"Once finding the letter, Harrison Grey did his own investigation, and learned that Charles had a hand in his father's death. That is why Charles Grey faked his own death and was on the run, afraid for his life. Harrison handed over the information to the magistrate prior to the masquerade. Nevertheless, the magistrate and I were able to apprehend him quietly. Your daughter, however, was not as quiet in her reentry back into society."

Evelyn defended herself, "Kenneth! You say that as if I had another choice!"

Silence saw her face go ashen, then immediately flush crimson. He laughed and shared a line from *Macbeth*. "'Thou cream faced loon. Where got'st that goose look?'"

Her pursed lips were adorable, because she was taking the bait. "'I was searching for a fool when I found you.' That was from *As You Like it.*" She turned to her sister and parents and said with a wink, "'There's a man that has more hair than wit'. He could have been famous performing that from of *A Comedy of Errors.*"

The room laughed, but she had not noticed that Silence had closed the gap between them and whispered behind her, "'Better a witty fool, than a foolish wit.' My dear, Evelyn, 'Your wit makes wise things foolish'. My heart could no more be yours than men could stop winter from coming."

Her stance softened, and she turned fully to him. He reached to embrace her, but clearly she was not done and quoted *Troilus and Cressida*: "'Thou crusty batch of nature.' But you are *my* crusty batch of nature. I could no more give myself to you any more than I already have. You will never be without me. Because, dear Kenneth, 'Your abilities are too infant-like for doing much alone.' You need me."

"That I do. You have made me a 'false and dull-eyed fool.'" *Merchant of Venice* was one of his staples. But he chose his own words next. "I would be lying if I did not tell you how anxious I am that we wed."

They finally embraced and he cradled her head to his chest, making the room disappear.

He had barely gotten a chance to ensure her safety, let alone understand how scared she must have been.

Her grip on him was more than just love. It was longing. It was need.

It was the same yearning and hunger he had for her.

"Yes, Papa, let us wed soon," Evelyn muffled into his chest, gripping the great coat more.

Mr. Hughes cleared his voice, stood to his full height, and concluded the Shakespearian flirtatious battle as he said to Evelyn, with clear absurdity, "'Get thee to a nunnery!'"

It was from *Hamlet* and left the room feeling slightly uneasy, witnessing such private affection, but also intense joy at seeing the full support that Mr. Hughes had truly meant. It was a stark difference in Mr. Hughes for sure. Not once had he asked about what Silence made in a year.

Again Mr. Hughes spoke and said, "Go, enjoy the gardens for a moment, and spare us the odd flirtations. You have already agreed to rescue her reputation with marriage. I just hope that society believes that Evelyn was in the country, privately courting the duke's friend, Mr. Silence.

"I do believe that is the only truth worth sharing that will not harm your standing in society," Mrs. Hughes said without being fully committed to the statement.

Kenneth spoke up, "Actually, I believe we could say that she hired the duke's friend to investigate something of great importance."

Evelyn smiled, and released her grip enough to reach for his face, cradling it in her hands and said, "We know the Duke of Huntsman will collaborate the story of how I was under his care, and that he advised me in buying the duke's silence."

She continued, "But the truth is, I fell in love with a man who both saw me for who I was and who I could be, at the same time. He accepted me in my entirety, and yet I know he will always push me to my potential. So even though there was no money exchanged I have paid the price, by fully trusting in love. The reward of trusting in love is that I have a powerful love in him. And that is worth any price."

THE END

Other books by Jeanna Ellsworth

Pride and Prejudice variations

Mr. Darcy's Promise
How can an honorable promise become so vexing?

Pride and Persistence
At some point, a good memory is a bad thing.

To Refine Like Silver *
Our trials do not define us; rather they refine us.

The Hope Series Trilogy:

Hope for Mr. Darcy *
Hope is all they have left, will it be enough?

Hope for Fitzwilliam *
For two destined to be together, hope is their only defense.

Hope for Georgiana *
Hope has become vital—*especially* when it comes to love.

Regency Romance

Inspired by Grace *
What started as friendship has evolved into something quite tangible.

Buying the Duke's Silence *
Eventually Evelyn learns that Mr. Silence is golden.

* Indicates Christian Romance

About the Author

Jeanna Ellsworth is so proud of her three daughters, who have supported her through her writing, and have always been her inspiration. She also proudly states she is the eighth of thirteen children, and firmly believes her parents taught her the skills she needed to succeed.

When she isn't blogging, gardening, cooking, or raising chickens—or more realistically, writing—she is thoroughly ignoring her house for a few hours at a time in order to read yet another romance novel, and does not feel guilty in doing so. She absolutely loves her chance to influence lives as a Nurse coordinator in an Organ Transplant Center. She finds great joy in her many roles she juggles, but writing especially has been her therapy.

Jeanna fell in love again with Jane Austen when she was introduced to the incredible world of Jane Austen inspired fiction. She can never adequately thank the fellow authors who mentored her and encouraged her to write her first novel.

She loves hearing from her readers and cherishes the chance to interact with them. For more information on her books and writing, please visit her website, www.HeyLadyPublications.com